LILLY

Mail-Order Brides of Cowboy Creek #3

JO GRAFFORD, WRITING AS

JOVIE GRACE

ISBN: 978-1-63907-038-1

Acknowledgments

Thanks so much to my editor, Cathleen Weaver, and an enormous thank you to my beta readers, Mahasani and Debbie Turner. I also want to give a shout out to my Cuppa Jo Readers on Facebook. Thank you for reading and loving my books!

Join Cuppa Jo Readers at https://www.facebook.com/groups/CuppaJoReaders for sneak peeks, cover reveals, book launches, birthday parties, reader games, and more!

Free Book!

Also, visit www.JoGrafford.com to sign up for my New Release Newsletter and receive your FREE copy of one of my sweet romance books!

Introduction

A *wildly independent spinster proprietress, a hunky blacksmith in the market for a bride, and the mail-order mistake that lands him in her boarding house for the holidays...*

Lilly Byrd has just been handed the keys to the Rose Haven Boarding House by the former owner who's determined to retire by Christmas. However, Widow Gable is concerned that the spirited bluestocking will use her new position as an excuse to continue dodging every potential beau who looks her way. So she puts a bug in the ear of Lilly's three matchmaking sisters, who are delighted to send the town's big and bearish new blacksmith her way to rent a room.

Orphaned in his early teens, Graham Christensen is happy to be hanging his shingle in Cowboy Creek and can't wait to settle down with a family of his own there. There's just one problem with his plan — the mail-order bride he sent for was misrouted to a different groom, and the agency claims it's too risky to send another bride west before the spring thaw. To make matters worse, the

1

construction company he hires is running several months behind schedule.

Thank goodness a room opens up at the highly sought-after Rose Haven Boarding House, which just so happens to be run by the loveliest, sassiest little spitfire Graham has ever encountered. He knows he's supposed to be waiting until spring to tie the knot with a mail-order bride he's never met, but the strong-willed, capable Lilly swiftly captures his attention and his heart. He's not discouraged to discover that she considers him to be just another pesky man she doesn't need in her life.

Fortunately, he has a few tricks up his large sleeves to prove just how useful it can be for a budding businesswoman to have a blacksmith to call her own.

Chapter 1: Wise Advice

LILLY

October, 1868

*I*t's all mine.

Lilly Byrd spun in a slow circle to absorb the warmth of the fire leaping in the hearth. It was the same parlor she'd stepped into at daybreak to begin her work day. It held the same pair of sofas covered in pale blue velvet, the same pinewood pianoforte polished to a full shine, and the same curtains framing the front picture window. They were white eyelet lace — handmade by the former proprietress, Martha Gable, or Widow Gable as the townsfolk preferred to call her.

It was the same boarding house, yet not the same boarding house because of one monumental change; Rose Haven now belonged to her. Or so its magnanimous giver claimed.

Lilly knew better, though. There had to be a catch. People never did anything without expecting something in return. There was always a catch.

Her fingers tightened around the iron key to the front

door. The weight of it felt so good in her hand. So right. She couldn't bear the thought of handing it back, yet that was exactly what she was going to do.

"Pray forgive me, but I can't accept it." Her gaze snapped back to the spritely older woman, who was tapping the toe of one black-laced boot and watching her with a smug sort of satisfaction. "It is too much."

"Too much work? Too much responsibility?" Martha Gable waved a hand airily at Lilly. "Well, speak up, child. I don't have all day to debate the particulars of our arrangement. You happen to be looking at the newly elected chairwoman of the Ladies Church Auxiliary." She spread the skirts of her violet wool gown in a mock curtsey. Her golden hazel eyes twinkled like two brilliant rays of sunshine.

Lilly studied her in troubled silence, finally understanding why her favorite boarding house proprietress was dressed with more care than usual this morning. She'd been busy running for office. The woman was always tackling a new project, forever on the lookout for her next big adventure.

"Well?" the widow prodded impatiently. "Are you going to congratulate me or not?"

Lilly nodded mechanically. "I'm very happy for you. You know that I am. I cannot imagine the church affairs being in better hands."

"On that we agree." The elderly woman smoothed a hand over her fluffy cloud of hair, mussing it further. It was naturally frizzy, impossible to contain in the bun she twisted it into each day. The resulting white wisps that curled and waved chaotically around her temples and cheeks merely added to her delightful brand of charm. "Being the right person for the job is exactly why I threw my hat into the ring, and exactly why the ladies of

4

Cowboy Creek had the good sense to cast their vote for me."

It wasn't shallow preening. As the widow of one of the town's founding fathers, she and the late Mr. Gable were among the biggest movers and shakers of Cowboy Creek. Her faithful constituents would follow her into battle. Her voice was one they would listen to until the last breath she drew.

"It's still no reason for you to give away your boarding house," Lilly returned calmly. It was probably the hardest thing she'd done in her life, but she held out her hand and uncurled her fingers. The iron key lay there, waiting for Widow Gable to take it back.

The woman gave it a languid wave. "Be that as it may, I cannot continue running the place myself. I have too many other responsibilities on my shoulders these days."

Lilly kept the key extended in her direction. "Then I will continue to run it for you. You pay me generously for the hours I serve here."

"Bah!" Widow Gable danced toward the front picture window, fluffing the curtains out of sheer habit. She nimbly reached up to tuck one of the panels more securely behind the brass ring holding it in place. "You'll become richer quicker if I just give the blasted thing to you — lock, stock, and barrel."

"You can't just give your business away." Lilly couldn't believe the woman was being so obtuse, and there was no way she was taking advantage of the kindhearted creature's temporary lapse in judgment.

"Why not?" the elderly woman spun around so suddenly that her skirts swirled around her ankles. "The boarding house is mine to do whatever I please with, and I choose to give it to you."

"I can never pay you back, ma'am."

"I'm not asking you to, lass. It's a gift with no strings attached."

"Why me?" Lilly stared at her in disbelief. "We're not even kin."

"Ah, that." A sad expression flitted across the older woman's face as she waggled a gloved finger in the air. "But you are as close to kin as I'll ever have."

Lilly blinked back the sting of tears. "And we will continue to be like kin, regardless. You do not need to give me Rose Haven to solidify our friendship, ma'am." They'd known each other for the better part of two years, during which time the widow had taught her everything there was to know about the boarding house business. Lilly had started off cleaning rooms and serving food, worked her way up to the front desk, and was eventually assigned to help out with the bookkeeping.

"Well, it is already done and cannot be undone." Martha Gable dusted her hands as if anxious to have the ordeal behind them. "I spoke with my attorney weeks ago. The deed has been transferred to your name and is locked inside the safe behind the pantry shelves. Rose Haven now belongs to you, whether you like it or not."

Lilly's mouth fell open. "But—"

The widow ignored her protest. "I shall continue to stay overnight, free of rent, anytime I wish."

"But of course!" Lilly gasped. "I would never dream of charging you rent." The dear woman and her husband had built the place from the ground floor up, and she'd already sold her mansion for a song and a dance to Lilly's favorite brother-in-law, Charley Arrington. He was married to her next older sister, Grace. Interestingly enough, Martha Gable had hired a construction company to remodel the old carriage house behind the mansion before the sale was finalized. It was where Lilly had been living with her mother and youngest sister, Magnolia — a comfortable and convenient arrangement that she'd long suspected was no accident.

Widow Gable gave a hearty cackle. "Well, you can dream about it all you want in the coming days, with my blessing, but you're still stuck with boarding me anytime I choose. It's in the fine writing. My attorney made sure of it."

Lilly squeezed her fingers around the iron key as she dropped her hand limply to her side. "I don't know what to say."

"You don't need to say anything." Her friend beamed merrily at her. "Knowing that I chose the right person to carry on the Gable legacy in this town is all the thanks I require."

"Where will you go?" Lilly blurted. It didn't sound as if her former boss intended to keep living in the main-floor suite at the back of the boarding house.

"Wherever I want," the woman responded vaguely. "Here and there. I may even hop on a train and do a little traveling." She turned, as if preparing to leave, then paused. "Oh, and I have a pair of lads coming today to move my things to a cozy little cottage on the edge of town."

"Of course you do," Lilly murmured. Every time she turned around, she was discovering that Widow Gable owned yet another building or piece of property.

"You'll need to keep sending those pots of stew down to the hungry lads at the livery," the woman continued as if she hadn't heard her.

"I certainly will."

"Selling the boarding house to a new owner would've never guaranteed things like that. You know it, and I know it."

Lilly's breath came out in a sigh of wonder. Greatly moved by the woman's words, she held out her arms.

Martha Gable moved across the parlor with a speed that belied her advanced years. The strength of her embrace never failed to amaze Lilly. The woman might be tiny, but everything about her packed a real wallop — her capable hands, her heart of gold, and her generous soul.

She abruptly pulled back, though she continued to clasp Lilly's shoulders. She had to crane her neck up at Lilly since she was several inches shorter. "I have one more favor to ask of you."

"Yes. Anything." Lilly didn't hesitate before answering. She trusted Martha Gable like she would have a flesh-and-blood grandmother.

"My sweet little bluestocking, do not use my gift to further harden your heart against the notion of falling in love someday."

Lilly's frame went stiff. "You've always welcomed plain speaking, ma'am, so I'll not be apologizing for choosing my career over marrying like my sisters did. I prefer to make my own way in life, not depend on some pesky man to provide for me." Her mouth twisted as she spoke. She knew with sudden certainty that she'd never voluntarily give up her newfound independence. It was too important, too precious.

The iron key she was currently clutching wasn't simply for locking and unlocking the doors of Rose Haven. It was going to put her on the path to financial independence. It was going to help her restore everything her family had lost during the war. Well, maybe not everything. Nothing would bring back her father and two brothers, but she'd see to it that her mother and youngest sister were taken care of. From now on, they'd want for nothing.

"I do welcome plain speaking, and I hope you'll

continue to welcome it from me in return." Mrs. Gable lifted her chin. "I know some folks in this town think I've already slid over the hill of eccentricity. My gift to you will only strengthen such theories. But the truth is, I didn't start off wealthy. I know what it feels like to be cold and hungry. And I certainly know what it means to be lonely. All the money my husband and I made together was never able to put a babe in my barren belly. And all the money in the world won't keep you warm at night. You'll find that out soon enough for yourself."

Her vehemence rendered Lilly momentarily speechless.

Widow Gable angled her head knowingly. "When the excitement of my gift wears off and the full burden of this business settles on your young shoulders, you might just find yourself longing for another set of shoulders to share the weight."

"No, I—"

"Just keep your heart open to the possibilities, child. That's all I'm asking."

Lilly couldn't imagine ever feeling lonely while running such a thriving boarding house. However, she did not wish to contradict the generous lady again.

"I'd like for you to give me your word on the matter." The older woman squeezed Lilly's shoulders for emphasis.

"My word?"

"That you will, in fact, keep your heart open to the possibilities."

Lilly gave a slight head shake. "I thought you of all people would understand my desire for independence." She was a modern woman and saw no reason to apologize for it.

"I do, lass."

"Someone has to stop my family's disastrous spiral into

poverty. The fact that I've chosen my career over marriage isn't something that I regret."

Martha Gable shrugged. "I'm not trying to talk you out of anything, least of all your freedom. I'm simply asking for you to keep your heart open to all the possibilities the good Lord may have in store for you."

"Which you think may include courting and settling down with a husband," Lilly muttered dully. *Surely you jest.* She had no interest in tethering herself to some cranky, controlling man who assumed a wife's role was to dote on his every need. She'd watched too many other women reduce their existence to little more than that. *I want more.*

"Nonetheless, I'll have your word, sweet girl, that you'll consider all the possibilities when the time comes." The widow held Lilly's gaze without blinking.

"Some of us were meant to be alone," she protested.

"Maybe for now," the woman returned evenly.

"Very well!" Lilly rolled her eyes. "I'll keep my heart and mind open. I will consider the possibilities with each and every pesky man who looks my way. Just know that I have every intention of turning down their foolish offers in the end."

"Good." Widow Gable's wide, expressive mouth stretched into a grin. "I've no desire to see you fall for any fools."

"So, that's it? I'm to consider the possibilities, eh?" Lilly sniffed, wondering why the woman had bothered securing her word for something so frivolous.

"Yes." Still grinning, the widow stepped back and fluttered her hand. "Well, I am off to storm the Ladies Auxiliary with a head full of ideas." She started ticking them off on her fingers as she faced the door. "There's so much to plan — our Christmas Tea, our pie fundraiser at the tree lighting ceremony, the gifts we'll be purchasing for the needy children in town…"

She paused by the hall tree to remove her favorite gray wool cape. Draping it around her slender shoulders, she nimbly fastened the clasp of the fluffy fur collar.

"It's only October," Lilly reminded. "You have plenty of time."

"That's what everyone always says," her friend scolded. "But I'm old enough and wise enough to know that Christmas always comes earlier than you expect. It seems eons away, then boom!" She clapped her hands together. "It's here. Every chairperson I've ever known has wished for twice the time and triple the funds to accomplish all they set out to do. That's why I plan to start now. I intend to be more ready for Christmas than all of my predecessors put together."

Lilly studied her worriedly as another thought struck her. She hoped the widow's frenzied level of energy wasn't motivated by a secret illness. Some folks really stepped up the pace of their lives when they sensed time was running out.

"Quit looking at me like that." Widow Gable made a face at her. "The rest of the town already thinks I'm a bit touched in the head. You know me better."

Lilly's feet churned into motion as relief flooded her chest. "Wait." She hurried to the door and threw her arms around the sweet little woman. "Before you go, I just want to say thank you. For everything."

"You're welcome." The elderly woman gently disengaged herself from Lilly's embrace and let herself out the door. "Just don't forget your promise. I'll be holding you to it."

Lilly stared after her, shaking her head, and returned to the front desk. She had a list of ingredients to finish writing up that would need to be purchased for the next week's worth of meals at the boarding house. She'd drop it off at the General Store right after lunch. The owner would have them added to Widow Gable's tab and delivered to the side entrance to the kitchen. *Er, my tab now.*

There was also a room upstairs that needed a floor-to-ceiling cleaning today. One of their longest-standing guests had vacated it only hours earlier. He was a rail worker who'd been employed all summer long by Lilly's other brother-in-law, David Pemberton. The retired Army captain, who was now married to her oldest sister, Elizabeth, was the sole reason the Byrd women had relocated from their hometown of Charleston. Elizabeth had answered his advert in the newspaper for a mail-order bride, and the rest of their family had traveled north to be with her soon afterward.

Lilly's nose curled at the memory of her conversation with the departing rail worker.

"I want a wife and a family, Miss Lilly. Alas, there aren't many women of marriageable age in Cowboy Creek. So unless you know of one…" He'd dangled his room key suggestively in the air before handing it to her.

"I do not." She'd all but snatched the key from him before writing out the receipt for his final rent payment. Rail workers were little more than drifters, moving from town to town wherever the next spur was being built.

She sighed at the memory as it dawned on her that Widow Gable might've gotten wind of their conversation, or been eavesdropping at the time.

You're right, ma'am. I didn't so much as consider the possibilities of marrying the likes of him. My answer to him would've been the same, though, if I had.

Another hour passed as she moved between the kitchen and front desk, alternating between stirring the pair of stewpots she had simmering and working her way through her daily bookkeeping tasks. She felt like she was walking in a bit of a daze, hardly able to believe that every floorboard she stepped on belonged to her now. Every carrot and potato in the pantry was hers, along with every table and chair in the dining room. Even the antique stool she was perched on behind the front desk with its swivel seat and ornately carved arms now belonged to her.

She was so awash with gratitude that it took an extra second to register the sound of the small brass bell that Widow Gable had rigged to jingle every time the front door opened.

Glancing up from the ledger she'd been poring over, Lilly found herself staring at the tallest, broadest bear of a man she'd ever laid eyes on. He had to stoop as he stepped over the threshold to avoid hitting his head on the door frame. It was an old building, so the doorways weren't as high or as wide as the newer buildings in town. However, they weren't exactly fairy-sized, either. His stooping meant he was seven feet tall or thereabouts.

As he strode in her direction, he removed a slouched leather Stetson and tucked it under one arm, causing a wave of wind-tossed auburn hair to fall over his forehead. The floorboards beneath her stool reverberated from the weight of his footfalls.

Oh. My. Lands! She nearly swallowed her tongue. Not only was he the biggest man she'd ever encountered, he was by far the handsomest. And there was something utterly mesmerizing about the way his green gaze was spearing hers. For a moment, she swayed atop the stool. Or maybe the dizziness was only inside her head. She had no way of knowing for sure. Not quite trusting her power of speech, she waited for the man to speak first.

Chapter 2: New Boarders

LILLY

"**G**raham Christensen." He thrust out one enormous paw. He wasn't wearing gloves, so there was nothing to hide the many scars crisscrossing the back of his hand. "I'm the new blacksmith in town."

Her eyes widened at the undeniable twang in his voice. "You're from the south." *Like me.* The words burst from her before she could call them back and were a far cry from the cultured greetings her mother had taught her and her sisters. Apparently, the cold northern temperatures had frozen the southern belle manners right out of her.

"I was born and raised in Savannah." The man's expression brightened as he continued to keep his hand suspended in the air. "And you?"

Possibilities. Consider the possibilities. Lilly forced a polite smile as she recalled Widow Gable's words. She accepted his hand. "My family is from Charleston, and I am pleased to meet you." *There.* She'd finally remembered her manners.

"The pleasure is all mine." His gaze glittered with interest as they shook hands — the male kind of interest.

"I'm Lilly Byrd, sir." She chose her words carefully, hoping to remind him that this was no social call. "How may I help you?" After working two years in a town of mostly men, she was accustomed to enduring and taming their exuberance at finding themselves in the presence of a woman.

She was far less accustomed to drowning in the rare evergreen hue of this man's twinkling gaze. Good gracious! Graham Christensen's eyes were as deep and as fathomless as the forests dotting the hills around them. They were polite, yet assessing, with an edge of something that Lilly's instincts told her could turn deadly if properly provoked. She stifled a shiver, a bit unnerved by his size, yet unwilling to give him the satisfaction of showing it.

He gave her a crooked smile that made her suck in a breath for no particular reason. It just did. His expression certainly wasn't the look a man would normally give a confirmed spinster like herself. She had on her plainest, most serviceable work gown today, a dove-gray wool with no frills other than the white embroidered collar she'd pinned on. And yet, there was something about being in his presence that made her feel a little less plain.

In the past, receiving such a flirtatious look from any man would have raised her hackles, but Mr. Christensen hadn't followed up the look with anything inappropriate. He wasn't hovering insufferably or saying anything that made her uncomfortable. In fact, he was showing all the signs of being a perfect gentleman, despite the over-whelming amount of space he took up.

"I need to rent a room, possibly for the entire winter." He gave a rueful snort. "The loft above our shop is in poor repair, and my apprentice and I aren't yet accustomed to breathing in icicles and exhaling frost."

His confession elicited a tug of sympathy laced with

homesickness. Two years of living in the west wasn't nearly long enough to make her forget the much warmer and balmier winters of Atlanta. Nonetheless, her lips parted at the thought that this hulk of a man wished to live under her roof for so many months. She wondered if his apprentice was another leather and denim-clad giant like him.

"I reckon my request to stay the winter sounds like a powerful long time," he added wryly. "Right now, however, it would solve a lot of problems for me. To put it more simply, everything that could go wrong on my first day in town, has."

"I am sorry to hear it, sir."

"I thought I'd planned every detail of our move before our arrival, but nothing has worked out like it was supposed to. To begin with, my mail-order bride got misrouted to another town, and the agency says they can't send another one until spring thaw."

Your mail-order bride, eh? His announcement was like a bucket of cold water cascading over Lilly. *Of course.* A charming southern man like Graham Christensen wouldn't stay single for long, not even in a town with so few women in the marriage market — not that it mattered. *I don't care. It's none of my concern.*

But she did care. *Drat you, Mrs. Gable, for the ridiculous promise you made me give you!* For some reason, considering the possibilities with the new blacksmith in town was enough to take Lilly's breath away. It had her thinking about things like how her tall beanpole frame would never tower over this particular man during a dance. It also had her thinking that she hadn't minded the press of his callused fingers against hers and that she would never tire of gazing into the green abyss of his eyes. They were questing with a hint of mystery, suggesting he had hidden depths in him just waiting to be explored. At the moment, they were also tinged with frustration.

"If that wasn't bad enough, I've been informed by the company that's supposed to be building my cabin that something went cattywampus with the construction. As best I can tell, it won't be ready to move into until spring." He paused to give a gusty exhale. "If your scowl means that my request to rent a room for the winter is something you need to run past the boarding house owner—"

"I am the owner," she cut in sharply.

"Oh." He inclined his head respectfully. "Pray accept my apologies for assuming otherwise. I was sent here by the seamstress next door to my shop, and I thought she mentioned the place was run—"

"By Martha Gable, yes," Lilly interrupted as the first sliver of suspicion worked its way through her insides. The only seamstress in town she knew about was her youngest sister, Magnolia, or Mags as she preferred to be called. Like their two older sisters, Mags was a hopelessly interfering matchmaker. It was all Lilly could do to dodge their daily attempts at pairing her off with one lonely rancher or another.

"Rose Haven only changed hands this morning," she explained through stiff lips. "I reckon word hasn't gotten around about it yet." But it would. Widow Gable wasn't known for skill in keeping secrets. She'd probably have the news to the four corners of town by day's end.

Which still didn't explain why Mags was sending the handsome new blacksmith Lilly's way. She could've easily sent him to the livery a few doors down where a lot of the hardworking men in town stayed, especially the bachelor ones. It would've been far cheaper for Mr. Christensen and his apprentice to bunk there with the half-dozen or so other patrons.

"We may be blacksmiths, ma'am, but my apprentice and I take baths and have good table manners. I assure you."

Lilly blinked. "I am not questioning your table manners, sir." Though she found his comment amusing, her answer came out more tart than she intended.

"Nor are you in any hurry to offer me a room," he sighed. "Does this mean there are no vacancies?"

"It does not."

"Meaning?" He arched one thick, auburn brow at her, a gesture that made her insides go all soft and gooey with some inexplicable emotion.

"A room came open just this morning." He was very lucky he'd walked through the door when he did. Rooms at the Rose Haven were in great demand. It would be filled before nightfall. Her youngest sister surely had known that. It was interesting that she was making such an effort to fill the opening with a man of her own choosing. The situation would bear watching, in the event Mags and their two older sisters were up to their matchmaking shenanigans again.

"I'll take the room if it's still available," he offered eagerly.

"I haven't had the time to clean it yet." Again, Lilly's tone was harder than she intended. It was such rotten luck that a truly interesting man had finally popped into their tiny, remote village, only to inform her that he was already pledged to be wed to someone else.

"Not to worry." Mr. Christensen sounded greatly relieved. "Dan and I are more than willing to help straighten the place up."

Dan. Your apprentice, I presume? "Well, I'm going to have to turn down your offer." She pretended to look down her nose at him, not an easy task given his impressive height. "I have a reputation to maintain here at Rose Haven that does not include turning over soiled linens and dusty window panes to my newest customers."

He raised his hands, clutching his Stetson in front of him in mock defense. "As your newest customer, I stand corrected. How soon will our room be ready?"

A wicked thought struck her. "By the end of the week, and not a second longer," she promised in a falsely smooth voice. It was only Monday.

His expression turned to such comical dismay that she laughed aloud. "Then again, if you're willing to make your down payment this morning to reserve the room, I could probably negotiate something with the proprietress to get you into it a bit sooner. As I mentioned before, I know her well."

For an answer, he dug in his pocket. "Pray inform her that I'm willing to pay double the going rate."

Her eyes widened. "I already said the room was yours. There's no need to start offering bribes, sirrah!" She was enjoying their conversation far more than she should have and was loath to end it.

"Call it what you want," he grimaced, "but I'll gladly pay whatever it takes to get us into that room tonight."

His burst of vehemence surprised her. "I was only jesting about Friday." She sensed there was a story behind his reaction to her teasing, a serious one.

"So I gathered." His upper lip twisted with humor. "Are you always this heartless, or do you reserve such treatment for hardened blacksmiths?"

Oh, how she liked the man! Just listening to him reminded her of sweet tea, molasses cookies, and the home she and her family had been forced to leave behind in Charleston. He was kind, like her father had been, and every bit as amusing as the brothers she missed so much.

But that was all he could ever be to her — a delightful new boarding house customer, since his hand was already spoken for.

Lilly forced her thoughts back to the business transaction brewing between them. "Your room will be ready by dinner time this evening." She swiftly wrote out the receipt for their standard down payment. "Though it does beg the question as to why you and your apprentice are in such a dashing hurry to lay claim to it. In the event my sister failed to mention it, they nearly always have extra bunks in the loft over the livery. They're cheap, too."

"I didn't come here looking for cheap, ma'am."

He looked so grim that she was taken aback. "I see." She didn't, of course. She had no idea what she'd said to erase his jovial smile.

He glanced away, making her wonder what it was about Rose Haven that fit the bill for whatever he was looking for.

She slid his receipt across the counter. "Here you go, Mr. Christensen." Her voice was much gentler this time. "Welcome to Rose Haven. Your check-in time isn't until after dinner, but you and your apprentice are more than welcome to drop by for lunch as well. It's my way of saying thank you for choosing this fine establishment over your other options." *And, yes. This is the treatment I reserve for hardened blacksmiths, apparently.* She couldn't recall offering a free meal to any other boarder before they moved into their room. Going forward, all the meals would be included in their rent.

The way his gaze lit at her words made her feel like the most successful businesswoman in the west. As he accepted the receipt, his work-roughened fingers brushed against hers, making her heart skip a beat.

She briefly closed her eyes, reminding herself that

enjoying the company of the town's new southern black-smith was something she could not afford to do again. In a few short months, he would be wed to his mail-order bride, while Lilly continued serving the townsfolk and their visitors with food and lodging. This was the life she truly wanted — one that would never require her to forfeit her independence, one that would lead her and her family to financial freedom. Moments like these were merely a distraction from her goals.

When Lilly reopened her eyes, she found Mr. Christensen watching her in a curiously knowing manner that made her heart skip yet another beat. *Mercy!* She blindly pushed around a few papers on the counter, wondering if it had been wise to throw in that free meal, after all.

Chapter 3: Rocky Start

GRAHAM

The moment his fingers touched Lilly Byrd's fingers, Graham felt the connection as strongly as he had when they'd first shaken hands. He was fairly certain the boarding house proprietress felt it, too, if the pink stain on her cheeks was any indication.

She quickly snatched her hand back and busied herself with pushing papers aimlessly around the cabinet. Graham hated the awkward silence that followed. For the life of him, he didn't know if he'd brushed her fingers on purpose or on accident. All he knew was that he'd wanted to hold her hand. He still did.

A foolish desire! Muffling a groan of self-chastisement, he ran a hand through his hair, probably sending the windblown locks in all directions. It hardly mattered. He was standing at the front desk of the Rose Haven boarding house to rent a room, not to impress a woman.

The only female he needed to impress was the one he'd already pledged to wed, a complete stranger that the mailorder bride agency would be sending his way next spring to replace the one they'd misrouted to Wyoming a week ago. How in the blazes had they made such an error? Wyoming wasn't spelled anything like Texas, so the mix-up made no sense to him and probably never would.

Before he'd made Lilly Byrd's acquaintance, the only bright spot in the situation was that his new bride would not have to endure a winter in a cramped boarding house room. Well, that, and he could now share his rented quarters with Dan Forest, which would prevent the man from being stuffed like a sardine with umpteen other cowboys in the livery stable loft.

Now that Graham had met Lilly Byrd, however, he was simply glad he wasn't yet married. He couldn't quite put his finger on what it was about her that interested him so much. It wasn't simply because she was southern, though he liked that fact enormously. She certainly wasn't trying to attract any attention to herself. Her no-frills gray gown made that clear enough, along with the simple twist her hair was pulled into. She wore no adornments, other than an intricately crocheted white collar, and she wasn't carrying on like a woman did when she was trying to impress a man. No, indeed. Lilly Byrd hadn't so much as batted her eyelashes at him. Not even once.

Nor did she need to. She was pretty enough without putting on airs. She possessed fine-boned features and a perfect creamy complexion, glossy blonde hair with those stray wisps that made a fellow long to reach over and smooth them back. Her striking blue eyes drew his gaze back to hers again and again.

Her very presence was intoxicating. Graham was drawn to her efficient hand movements, as well as her pretense of being absorbed in her paperwork. Her utter lack of simpering and flirting was all the more noticeable, since his gut told him she was as aware of him as he was of her.

It was a sentiment she showed no signs of acting on. *More's the pity!* Graham couldn't help wondering if it had something to do with her upbringing. Her cultured accent and ladylike manner suggested that she'd been raised in a very different environment than the work-a-day one she currently inhabited. If he had to venture a guess, he'd say he was conversing with an impoverished gentlewoman. It was a common tale in the war-torn south. It also meant that she very likely didn't view him as a social equal. He was a customer to her and nothing more, certainly not a man to be wooed or courted.

Again, Graham inwardly scolded himself for the direction of his thoughts. He was the world's biggest fool for entertaining such outrageous ideas, especially when he was already pledged in writing to wed another woman. He searched for something to say that would restore the conversation to their previous lighthearted banter. It was time to end the encounter and take his leave.

"I sure do appreciate the fact that you have a room to rent." Graham rested an elbow on the check-in booth and leaned forward on it to bring himself to her eye level. His movements inadvertently brought their faces closer together, making Lilly Byrd blush all over again. By all that was great and good, the lass was downright lovely when she blushed.

This time, she didn't pull away from him, which both surprised and charmed him. It also infused him with hope-less longing — to spend more time with her and to get to know her better, both of which were highly inadvisable.

"Oh, but that is no longer the case, sir." She straightened the papers she'd been fiddling with into a single stack. Then she tapped the one on top that he'd just finished signing. "According to this document, my boarding house is completely full again. Well, except for the one small room I keep handy downstairs for quick, overnight stays."

Realizing she was referring to his reservation, he grinned. "If I was any other fellow, I'd probably tell you it's my lucky day. Might even credit my good fortune to the lucky boots I chose to wear here."

It tickled him to no end when curiosity got the better of her. She rocked forward on her hands to peek over the cabinet. He couldn't help catching a whiff of her flowery scent. Rosewater, if his sniffer was working properly. Some days he spent so much time at his forge that all he could smell was smoke and melting metals.

She straightened and wrinkled her nose at him. "It looks to me like you're wearing regular ol' boots."

She was taller than the average woman, but she was still a petite thing compared to him. If he rounded the cabinet and stood face-to-face with her, the top of her head would just barely reach his shoulder.

"That's because they are regular ol' boots. I was merely jesting. Never did put much stock in random luck. I'm more a man of faith."

"Oh?" Her rosy lips quirked in such a warm smile that he felt like he was bathing in pure sunshine. Did that mean she was a person of faith, too?

"Yes, I believe things happen for a reason. Our meeting, for instance."

Her clear, assessing gaze turned contemplative. "You truly think it's more than a coincidence that you stepped through my front door to claim my last available room?"

"Indeed, I do. It appears that Dan and I were meant to stay a spell at Rose Haven."

She shook her head, looking bemused. "Then you must also believe your would-be bride was meant to become lost."

He chuckled. "What I believe is that a very lovely boarding house proprietress is having a bit of fun at my expense."

"Or maybe a certain blacksmith is chuckling up his oversized sleeves at my expense," she returned cheekily.

"Never!" he shot back. "I wouldn't dream of poking fun at a lady, especially not a lady with the power to toss me and my apprentice without mercy into the street."

Her silky blonde brows arched in faux confusion. "I highly doubt I am capable of tossing you any distance, sir, no matter how hard I might try."

He snorted, tickled beyond belief at her humorous reference to his size, though he was fast growing tired of being called Mister and Sir by her. He appreciated the respect she was treating him with, but he knew with sudden certainty that this was a lass he'd rather be on a first-name basis with.

"Yes, indeed," he drawled lazily, "you are most certainly having fun at my expense."

She spread her hands. "You're the one who said everything happens for a reason. I am merely curious as to how a misrouted bride fits into the picture."

He shrugged, thoroughly enjoying the fact that Lilly Byrd found his unwed state a topic of interest. "I think the answer is obvious. She was meant to marry someone other than me." There. It was a relief to finally get that troubling thought off his chest. Even more troubling was the fact that he was no longer disappointed about the agency's mistake. He'd stopped being disappointed the moment he'd walked into Rose Haven.

Lilly nodded, though she still looked doubtful. "All jesting aside, sir, I fail to see how sending off for a mail-order bride demonstrates one's faith. From my perspective, it looks more like gambling."

Graham's brows shot upward at her plain speaking. He'd not expected such honesty or such censure from a complete stranger. "Well, when you put it like that," he shook his head ruefully, "I reckon I can't argue the matter." *Lord, have mercy!* He clearly had some praying to do when he got back to his shop. So much for his shameless bragging about being a man of faith. It had taken the outspoken boarding house proprietress only a handful of seconds to point out how his actions indicated the opposite was true.

Guilt shot through his gut at the thought that maybe he'd been too hasty to take things into his own hands when it came to finding a bride. For one thing, the rumor that there were no marriageable women in Cowboy Creek was clearly false. On his first day in town, he'd already met two of them — two completely lovely and infinitely appealing southern belles who were ripe for courting.

Their single state was a bit odd, though, considering how many bachelors lived and worked nearby. What was wrong with these western fellows? Did they consider southern girls beneath their notice? Or was there some other reason the two sisters weren't yet wed? Perhaps they were embroiled in some sort of scandal, though that didn't seem likely, considering that both of them ran thriving businesses. It probably wouldn't hurt to do some asking around, though, just in case — at least for Dan's sake.

His apprentice was equally interested in finding a wife to settle down with, though he didn't possess the funds to send off for a mail-order bride like Graham had. Maybe it was a good thing Dan couldn't afford such a service, especially if Lilly Byrd's assessment of it was correct. Did paying to skip the courting process truly indicate that his faith in God was weak? He sure hoped not. The bridal agency owner had been bubbling with testimonies about all the successful matches they'd made in the past year alone, including several right here in Cowboy Creek.

Regardless, Graham planned to take a closer look at his copy of the mail-order bride contract before bedtime. It wouldn't hurt to find out what it would take to cancel the contract in the event the good Lord had something else planned for him here in Cowboy Creek.

Which he suddenly and mightily hoped was the case…

Graham found Dan hefting supplies from their rented wagon that was parked at the curb. It was full of the tools and supplies they'd traveled with on the train from Georgia. The dusty cowboy stomped past Graham on his way back inside their new shop.

"You picked a perfect time to be gone, boss." His sarcastic tone indicated that his true feelings ran in the opposite direction.

"But a far less perfect time to return," Graham shot back. "If I'd stayed away another ten minutes, you'd have had the whole wagon unloaded." He hoisted their biggest anvil from the wagon before following Dan inside. It weighed nearly two hundred and fifty pounds, so he didn't continue speaking until after he'd set it down in the middle of their shop. *Whew!* The anvil seemed to get heavier each time he lifted it. He straightened and dusted his hands.

"Show off!" Dan shot him a dark look from the rafter he was standing beneath. He'd hammered in a series of nails from which he was hanging a full array of tools — hammers, punches, and chisels. On the wall shelf beneath them, he'd neatly arranged their wedges, forms, and fullers. "You arrived just in time to lift the heaviest item all by yourself."

"Aw," Graham mocked. "Did I steal your opportunity to flex your pipes for the purty gal next door?" He hated how threadbare and faded Dan's shirt and coat were getting. If only the fellow would listen to reason and quit refusing Graham's offer to buy him a new set of work clothes. The one and only outfit he'd accepted from Graham last Christmas, he wore strictly to church services. Meanwhile, he continued to mend and patch the rags he wore around the shop. Someday soon they were going to fall clean off his wiry frame.

"Ha!" Dan's sandy blonde brows flew skyward. "She took one look at me and her nose went so high in the air, it'll be a miracle if she doesn't drown during the next rainstorm."

"What?" Graham protested. "I found her to be both pleasant and welcoming."

"To you, maybe," Dan muttered. "Folks like her know they've got to get in good with the blacksmith. That way you'll be at her beck and call the next time she needs you to fix something. But me? I'm just the lowly apprentice. Useful for fetching things and otherwise kicking to the curb."

Whoa! Graham's gaze narrowed in contemplation as he watched Dan straighten a few wedges. "I'm mighty glad she thought to mention the vacancy at the boarding house," he noted mildly.

"Right." Dan's mouth twisted bitterly. "Wonder if she would've even bothered if she knew I'd be sharing the room."

"Did something happen between the two of you in my absence?" Graham crossed his arms and waited, hoping his apprentice hadn't done anything to offend their next door neighbor. Dan Forest could be a bit of a hothead at times, but Graham had never before seen him treat a lady with anything less than respect.

Dan whirled around, his freckled features livid with outrage. "Indeed. She said she wanted to mend my shirt."

Graham chuckled. "The nerve of her! She should be hog-tied and roasted for sparing you such kindness."

Dan snatched up the fire poker and bent to viciously stir the flames in the hearth. "Told her I couldn't afford her uppity services."

"Please assure me you did not employ the word uppity while addressing her," Graham groaned.

"I did not." Dan's face was beet red when he straightened. "Just said I didn't have the coin to spare, and that's when she…" He broke off his tirade and settled into frigid silence as he reached for the next box of supplies.

"When she did what?" Graham prodded. He reached for another box, which turned out to be full of their custom-made punches. He and Dan used them to bore holes in all sorts of items, from the handles of kitchen utensils to the nail holes on horseshoes.

Dan abandoned his unpacking to stomp across the room and straighten their collection of iron and steel rods. This was the raw inventory they used to melt down and craft new items. Graham fully expected to make more horseshoes than anything else in a town this far west of Savannah, where he and Dan hailed from. They'd grown weary of trying to eke out a living in the war-torn south and had decided to venture west to greener pastures.

"She offered to mend my shirt for free, that's what," Dan exploded.

Graham failed to see the problem. "Would you like me to report her to the sheriff for her insolence?"

"You're missing the point," Dan muttered.

"Then enlighten me."

"I'm not a charity case." Dan yanked a hammer down from the wall and viciously sent it into a pair of boards.

"Never said you were."

"Well, her words clearly indicated that's what she thinks I am. So did her highfalutin gown and prim-and-proper manner." Dan produced a handful of nails and pounded them home. In no time, a short square fence took shape from the boards he was hammering together. "That figures!" he huffed. "First pretty girl I run into is a blasted southern belle who thinks she's better than the rest of us."

The next whack he gave the boards was so loud it was a wonder they didn't split in two.

"Dare I ask what you're trying to kill over there?" Graham teased.

"It's a free-standing rack." Dan stood back to assess his work through narrowed lids. "This shop is considerably bigger than our last one, so I thought it might be nice to display our tongs this way."

Graham nodded. "I like it."

"Not bad for a lowly apprentice, eh?" Dan still sounded miffed.

"I think you're right about the impoverished status of the Byrd sisters." Graham was willing to give his friend that. "I'm not convinced they think they're better than us, though."

"Maybe because the hoity-toity Miss Magnolia didn't eye your shirt with disdain and offer to mend it for free," Dan growled. He returned his hammer to its hook.

"I've been offering to replace your shirt for months," Graham reminded. "You've never accused me of being highhanded or mean-spirited."

"Because you're not," Dan snarled. "You have good intentions even when you're being interfering."

"I'm going to take that as a compliment even though it

sounded like an insult." Graham was having a hard time trying not to laugh. The thought had just crossed his mind that the real reason Miss Magnolia Byrd had crawled so far under the skin of his apprentice had nothing to do with her unfortunate offer to mend his shirt. Wouldn't it be something to discover that his short-tempered apprentice had fallen head-over-heels for a woman he considered out of his reach? That would certainly explain all of his snapping and snorting.

He started to whistle beneath his breath.

Dan's head swiveled in his direction. "What are you so happy about?"

"I got us a room at the boarding house." Graham hid a grin. "It's run by Miss Lilly Byrd. Sounds like she's the sister of our lovely seamstress next door."

"Say it isn't so," Dan groaned.

"Our room will be ready by dinner time, but she said we could head over there for lunch if we wanted."

"See what I mean?" Dan waggled his finger. "I'm telling you, both of those women view us as charity cases."

"Or customers," Graham countered, "which we now are." At Dan's stony silence, he continued, "I don't particularly care what her reasons were for offering to feed us. The boarding house was clean, and the air smelled like fresh-baked bread and something good simmering on the stove. Come high noon, I'm marching myself down there and taking her up on her offer, whether you like it or not."

Dan let out a huff of air. "Fresh-baked bread?" he repeated in a hopeful voice.

"Or biscuits." Graham hid another grin as Dan's stomach growled. "Think you could suffer through the attentions of yet another beautiful southern woman long enough to join me for lunch?"

"I have no idea what you're talking about." Dan's voice

was nonchalant. "I'm fine. Don't reckon I have to like Miss High-and-Mighty next door to stay in her sister's boarding house."

"If by fine, you mean you find Miss Magnolia Byrd ten shades of lovely, and the discovery has your tail feathers in a terrible tangle, then yes. You're fine."

"I take back what I said earlier." Dan's upper lip curled. "You're as mean as a rattlesnake."

Graham started to whistle again. "Here and I thought I was finer than frog hair split four ways."

"Whatever you say, boss." Dan snorted. "While you stew in all that cock and bull, I'm heading out to return the wagon and horses to the livery. The poor beasts probably have icicles growing from their muzzles by now."

Graham gave him a mock salute, not bothering to defend himself. He was too busy counting the minutes until lunch time, and it wasn't merely because of the promise of a home cooked meal. For reasons he wasn't yet ready to explore, he couldn't wait to lay eyes on the sharp-tongued Lilly Byrd again.

Chapter 4: Key to a Man's Heart

GRAHAM

A t a quarter 'til noon, Graham paused his unpacking to wash his hands and face in the basin of chilly water against the wall. "Good gravy!" He toweled off. "It's only October, and already it's as cold as a wet hen that lost her way and ended up at the North Pole."

Dan, who'd transferred their vast collection of tongs to his newly built square gate, glanced over at him. "One of the fellas at the livery claims it smells like snow outside, whatever that means."

Graham sniffed the air. "I wasn't aware snow had a smell." Snow was merely frozen water, wasn't it? If it had a scent, though, he was anxious to get a whiff of it. Despite his lack of fondness for the diving temperatures, he was very much looking forward to witnessing his first real snowstorm. A southern boy through-and-through, he'd not experienced more than a dusting of it back home. It only snowed once every few years in Savannah, and it usually melted and was gone by the afternoon.

"Me, either." Dan shrugged as he headed for the washbasin. "Maybe it's just some odd western saying that means something else."

"Not at all." Lilly smiled merrily at Graham and Dan as she delivered a tray to their table a half hour later. She proceeded to set a brimming bowl of stew in front of each of them. "When the locals say they smell snow, they mean their noses have picked up on a winter storm headed our way. There's a special crispness in the air that you'll soon learn to recognize."

Dan nodded at her, looking fascinated. "I'll be sure to give the air an extra sniff when we return outdoors." Then he returned his attention to his stew. "Right now the only thing I can think about is lunch." He looked ready to break into tears of sheer happiness.

"Eat your fill. There's plenty more in the stewpot in the kitchen," she assured. "I'll be back shortly with a refill on your tea and another basket of bread rolls."

"You were right," Dan admitted as she glided away. "She's a lot nicer than her sister."

"I didn't say that." Graham glanced around the crowded dining room as he spooned his stew, amazed at how packed the place was. According to Lilly Byrd, Rose Haven contained a total of six guest rooms upstairs and one small broom closet-sized spot downstairs for those who were just passing through for one night. It meant the men in the room, who were gobbling down her bread and stew as fast as she could serve them, weren't all renters. There were a lot of other townsfolk mixed in with them — regular customers, it appeared. They were lounged comfortably in their high-back chairs, chatting a mile a minute with their tablemates.

The green and white checkered curtains framing the dining room windows were neatly pressed and tied back with red ribbons, hinting of the upcoming holidays while adding a homey feel to the room.

"She's dressed a lot more sensibly, too." Dan gave a grunt of gratitude as he slurped his way through his first bowl of stew.

"What are you talking about?" Graham scowled at his apprentice, sensing another gripe session was forthcoming.

"Miss Lilly Byrd. She's not decked out like some fancy queen about to hold court."

"Like her sister, eh?" Graham rolled his eyes, wishing his friend would give the topic a rest.

Dan nodded. "Did you get an eyeful of all that lace and gauze? It was enough to give me a headache."

Graham shrugged. "I'll admit she was outfitted a bit fancy for this town, but she's a seamstress, after all. Maybe it's her way of displaying her products to prospective customers."

"I hadn't thought of that." Dan shook his head, still looking disapproving. "Regardless, I prefer the way her sister is dressed."

The side entrance to the dining room opened, ushering in a blast of wind and eliciting a groan from those seated nearby. The groan was quickly replaced with whistles and shouts of greeting.

"Mags!" One of the lads from the livery waved wildly at Magnolia Byrd as she sailed into the room. "We was saving a seat fer ya!"

"How very kind of you!" She waved gaily in his direction but kept walking. A scarlet cape was wrapped snugly around her ruffled gown, and a matching wide-brimmed hat was tipped sassily over one side of her forehead. Frothy white ribbons cascaded from its brim.

"Great jumping bullfrogs!" Dan muttered, hunkering a

little further over his bowl of stew. "She sure does know how to make an entrance."

Though he glowered at her over the top of his spoon, Graham noted that the gaze of his apprentice followed the progress of their newest arrival across the room.

She nearly collided with her sister as the boarding house proprietress re-entered the room, both arms loaded down with bread baskets.

"Mags!" Lilly Byrd squealed in alarm.

"Lilly-bug!" the younger woman mocked, though there was no mistaking the affection behind her teasing. Without taking the time to remove her hat or cape, she swiftly divested her sister of half the baskets. They delivered them laughingly to the tables, stopping to exchange quick pleasantries with each cluster of townsmen.

"I thought you promised to call on me yesterday, lass," a grizzled older man chided in an affectionate voice to Miss Magnolia. "I waited up nearly half the night and went to bed brokenhearted."

The men sitting at his table dissolved into guffaws.

"Did I?" She arched her blonde brows playfully at him. "I'll have to check my calendar when I get back to the shop. I'm more inclined to think you're just trying to cut higher in line for getting your overalls mended."

The man struck a pose of mock offense with one heavily lined hand pressed to his shabby shirt. "Well, I swan, Miss Magnolia! I didn't know you had it in you to be so cruel."

She shook a finger in warning. "You're forgetting I have three sisters, Sam. I can spot a tall tale a mile away with my eyes closed. Speaking of miles away..." She paused her delivery of bread baskets, looking wistful. "How is that precious niece of mine? I haven't been able to ride out and visit her for too many days to count. What a horrible aunt I'm turning out to be!"

"I'll drive you!" a chorus of male voices offered.

Her smile was sad. "Thank you kindly, but none of your shirts and trousers will get patched and mended before spring if I accept all your offers."

She received many assurances from the hopeful men that they'd gladly go without, so long as she agreed to let them escort her to the captain's house.

"She's flirting with the entire room at one time and playing them all," Dan grumbled beneath his breath. "What a heartless tease!"

Graham didn't respond, since he didn't find Miss Magnolia Byrd's behavior the least bit offensive. From his perspective, she was simply being friendly. It wasn't her fault that a room full of men found her beauty and wit so irresistible. He noted that she was careful to keep her responses to their teasing brief, and she spared no more than a few seconds of attention to any one person at a time.

The man called Sam waited until the loudest young men finally quieted down before answering. "Your little niece is spoiled rotten, Miss Magnolia, and you know it. Though I'd take a bullet for her anytime, anywhere — make that a hundred bullets — the main reason I drove here to lunch was to steal a few moments of peace from her incessant demands."

A blinding smile lit Magnolia's features at his words. "Oh, how I miss the little rascal," she sighed. Then her smile slipped as she faced Sam again. "I deposited a gift for her in your saddlebag. If you see to it that she gets it, I might just finish mending your overalls ahead of schedule."

"And if I forget?" He winked at her.

"Then I might accidentally use pink thread on your overalls instead of blue."

Her words were met with a round of snickers from their listeners. Without waiting for a comeback from her grizzled conversation partner, Miss Magnolia whirled in the direction of Graham and Dan's table.

"My apologies for the delay in delivering your bread rolls, gentlemen." She set the final basket of bread on their table with a flourish. "I'm sure you overheard the nonsense I had to wade through on my way here."

Though none of the other men in the room had stood when she approached their tables, out of sheer habit, both Graham and his apprentice shot to their feet. They hadn't been gone from Savannah long enough to lose their old-fashioned southern manners in the presence of a lady.

Unless Graham's ears deceived him, a soft sigh of appreciation escaped her.

"Please have a seat." He waved her into his chair.

"Gladly. I thank you." To his surprise, she accepted his offer.

He motioned for Dan to return to his seat, which he did with great reluctance. Then Graham reached for his bowl of stew and lounged against the wall with it in his hands.

"I can't tell you how good it is to have a few more fellow southerners in town," she confessed in low tones. "The folks in Cowboy Creek are generous and kindhearted to a fault, but it's not the same as home, is it?"

Dan scowled at her. "I don't miss the orphanage where I grew up, if that's what you're asking."

Her lips parted in a gasp of astonishment. "Pray forgive me! I had no idea you'd endured such hardships."

"Of course you didn't." Graham shot his apprentice a warning glare. "And you are entirely right about missing the sunshine and hospitality of the south. My thin-skinned assistant over there was just a few minutes ago blubbering about how he might never get warm again."

"Blubbering?" Dan raised one sandy brow at his boss. "Here and I thought your elephant-sized teeth were chattering too loudly for you to hear anything over them."

Magnolia Byrd glanced between them with interest. "You truly have the patience of a saint," she cooed at Graham.

He blinked in astonishment. "I do?"

"Yes, indeed. If I had an apprentice who spoke to me the way yours does, I'd shred his backside with my sheers, then sew the rest of his britches to the nearest bucking bull with his sorry self still inside them."

Dan's face burned hot with anger. "Well, I reckon snipping holes in the nearest innocent male is one way for a seamstress to drum up business."

She blinked a few times. Then, to Graham's enormous relief, she laughed. "I don't know who licked the red off your candy, cowboy, but I know it's your first day in town, so I'm going to overlook your crankiness just this once. Not to mention your very nice boss obviously sees something good in you, or he wouldn't have dragged you kicking and screaming so far west."

Graham chuckled. "You sure nailed the cranky part, but you're right about the other, too. This hothead is a highly skilled blacksmith in the making."

Dan's hard jaw relaxed.

"Where some men only see a lump of iron, he sees the spokes of a wagon wheel or the shoes for an entire team of horses. I've watched him create something out of nothing so many times that I probably take his talent for granted most days."

Dan glanced away from the table, with a myriad shades

of red creeping up his neck. "I've learned everything I know from the best blacksmith in the country," he returned quietly. Then he lifted his gaze to their lovely guest. "It's a messy, dirty business, which is why hardworking men like me don't mind looking like scarecrows in our work clothes. Not everyone has the luxury of prancing around like royalty in silk britches while they labor."

Her chin came up. "You use the tools of your trade; I use the tools of mine, Mr. ah…I don't believe I caught your surname."

"It's Forest, ma'am, though you're more than welcome to call me Dan like everyone else. That is, unless fraternizing with a lowly apprentice is beneath you."

"My friends call me Mags," she shot back, "but since you're the least friendly fellow I've ever encountered, you may call me Magnolia. It'll tickle me to no end to imagine the physical pain you'll experience every time you refer to me as the most beautiful flower in the south."

The animosity between them was so thick by now that Graham winced. "So, er, Miss Magnolia…" He glanced helplessly around the room, trying to think of something to diffuse the situation before it got out of hand.

"Mags," she corrected sweetly. "As I've mentioned before, my friends call me Mags."

"I'd like that, Mags. Please call me Graham while you're at it." As Dan bristled, Graham plunged onward. "I just wanted to make one thing clear. If you and your sister ever have need of our blacksmith services, do not hesitate to give us a holler. We'll be sure to give you the boarding house discount on top of the southern belle discount on top of the—"

"Real blacksmith projects and repairs," Dan interrupted coldly. "To be clear, we don't service pins and needles and the like."

"You don't say," she mocked. "Very well. I'll be sure to only trouble you with sharpening and repairing my vast collection of scissors. I own more than a dozen." She held up a finger. "Oh, and my irons. I own ten of them, as well. Then there's my…" She went on to list a good six or seven other household items. Long before she was finished, Dan was gnashing his teeth.

"My offer still stands about mending your shirt, too." She wrinkled her nose at the garment as if she found it offensive. "For the next-door neighbor discount, of course. I don't see why we can't barter and trade favors instead of exchanging cash."

"We're blacksmiths, not fishwives," Dan reminded in a low voice.

Enough! Graham stepped between them. "That's a marvelous idea. We accept your offer, and Dan will have his threadbare shirt to you in the morning."

Magnolia leaned sideways to shoot a gloating look around him at his apprentice. "I'll do my best to resurrect the poor garment before it dissolves into a pile of lint and buttons."

"That's what hardworking men do," Dan taunted. "We wear out our threads."

"Fortunately for you, this hardworking woman knows how to knit them back together," she returned with false sweetness.

Just as Graham was about to throw his hands up in despair over his bickering companions, her tone dropped to a conspiratorial note. "Oh, and Graham, you'd best come to me about any repairs that need to happen here at Rose Haven. Lilly is new at running a boarding house, so I guarantee you'll be butting into her pride and independence every time you offer to help out."

"Duly noted." His lips twitched.

"I should probably also warn you that she's a confirmed spinster, which means she finds men in general to be pesky creatures."

Though Graham's heart sank at the news about Lilly's spinsterhood, he chuckled. He vowed on the spot to prove the sassy proprietress wrong. Men like him could be very useful to have around. She'd soon find out.

Over the next several days, Graham found himself falling deeper and deeper beneath the boarding house owner's spell. Lilly Byrd turned out to be so much more than a sharp-tongued bluestocking. Yes, she was outspoken, but she was also practical and fair-minded. Rose Haven purred along smoothly beneath her careful management. The fires in the hearths stayed lit, the food in the kitchen kept coming, and the windows and floors remained spotless.

A man could grow used to having a soft pillow beneath his head each night and the scent of baking bread in his nostrils each morning. He could also get used to having a capable, attractive woman tending to his comfort.

They crossed paths in the stairwell and the hallways, the dining room and the parlor. And every time their eyes met, he experienced the same jolt of awareness. They continued to dance around each other thus from October to November.

At first, Graham fought his growing attraction to her. Eventually, he came to realize it wasn't something he could fight. He was falling for Lilly Byrd, and that was that.

He spent many a night poring over his mail-order bride contract, trying to decipher the meaning behind all the complicated legal phrases it contained. He finally gave up and sent a telegram to the agency, informing them that he wished to cancel their agreement. There was no need to send him another bride come spring. He'd fallen in love with someone else. It was only a matter of figuring out when to break his silence on the topic and how to convince her to start courting him.

Before he could commence his plan for winning her heart, however, something truly horrible happened.

Dan banged open the door of the blacksmith's shop the evening before Thanksgiving. "You are not going to believe this," he seethed.

Graham glanced up from his forge. "Give me one minute to finish this. I'm nearly through."

He swung his hammer through the air, pounding the red hot edge of the plough handle he was repairing for a rancher on the edge of town. Since it was off season, he and Dan had been experiencing a flood of orders for farm tool repairs. Now was the time to re-attach rake prongs, replace shovel handles, shore up loose wheel spokes, and sharpen blades of all shapes and sizes.

"Alright, then." He pounded the plough handle for the last time, then rocked back on his heels to observe the finished product. He nodded in satisfaction. The handle was exactly the right length and shape. It was finished. "I'm all ears. What news do you have that I'm not going to believe?"

"You're not going to like it, either, so brace yourself."

Graham shot him a curious look as he returned his hammer to its hook on the wall. "Consider me braced. Out with it!" he urged impatiently.

"A very wealthy gentleman from Charleston stepped off the stagecoach an hour ago to pay a surprise visit to the Byrd family. His name is Lee Davenport, and he's made it clear that he plans to wed one of the sisters before Christmas."

Graham's head jerked away from the row of hammers he'd been examining. "Marry one of them?"

"You heard me, boss."

"From my understanding, the Byrd sisters left Georgia more than two years ago. I think we would've caught wind of any long-distance courtships by now. Small towns have a way of giving up even the deepest and darkest of secrets."

Dan spread his hands. "There's no secret courtship. He means to woo them right out in the open."

"Why? What's his angle?" Graham demanded.

"He claims he recently acquired the Byrd sisters' childhood home and insists it's only right to reinstate one of them as its mistress."

No! Fear prickled inside Graham's chest. He'd not yet launched his own bid to win Lilly's heart, but maybe it was already too late. How could a mere blacksmith compete with that?

"I warned you," Dan intoned in a low voice. "I knew all along that the Byrd sisters' friendship with us was too good to be true. Give a southern belle a chance to return to her throne, and she'll choose her crown every time over the poor saps who thought she truly cared about them."

Graham didn't want to believe the sassy, forward-thinking Lilly Byrd was capable of anything so crass. However, he decided to test her to be sure. He waited until he caught her alone in the kitchen to launch his plan.

"I'm going to miss my favorite boarding house proprietress after she leaves town." He strode across the room to stir the coals in her fire and turn the trio of hens she had roasting on spits.

"Indeed?" she returned dryly. "Since I am the only boarding house owner in town, I can also presume I am

45

your least favorite one, which means you will not miss me at all."

His heart sank at her words. Did it mean she'd already made up her mind to accept Mr. Lee Davenport's offer of marriage? "Then you would be wrong," he said quickly, "because the thought of you leaving town fills me with nothing short of despair."

"Why, Graham!" She paused her kneading, holding her floury fingers suspended over the ball of dough. She stared at him across her preparation counter. "Who said anything about me leaving town?"

"You did, when you wrongfully claimed I would not miss you."

"Only because I thought we were speaking in hypotheticals." Her creamy cheeks flushed such an enticing shade of rose that they stole his breath.

"Then you are not marrying Mr. Davenport and heading to Charleston with him?"

"I do not know." She sounded perplexed. "Like you, I made some promises recently."

He staggered and had to press a hand against the mantle to steady himself. "What sort of promises?" Horror filled his lungs at the possibility that she'd already accepted the man's offer.

"The woman who gifted me this boarding house made me promise to consider all the possibilities before turning down my next offer to court or marry." Lilly dropped her gaze and started fiddling with the dough again. "She doesn't understand my longing for independence or the financial security it will bring my family. She doesn't understand that so long as I remain unwed, this business and all of its income can never be taken from us by an unscrupulous male relative."

"Ah." He exhaled slowly, absorbing her words. "So you *are* considering Mr. Davenport's offer."

"Of course I am," she announced shrilly. "For all intents and purposes, I promised Widow Gable that I would."

"Even though it would force you to give up your independence?"

"Even though," she returned crisply. "Not that it's any business of yours, but it's not merely my own happiness at stake. Mr. Davenport is offering to place my mother back in her home by Christmas."

"Meaning you would sacrifice your dreams and goals to make her happy."

"In a heartbeat." There was no hesitation in her response.

"Is that what your mother wants?"

"She refuses to answer the question, insisting I should follow the Lord's will and whatever my heart is telling me, but of course it's what she wants."

Graham had never seen her more agitated. "What do you want?" he asked in a low voice.

"I don't know," she whispered. "I thought I did, but I don't. It's all such a muddle in my head right now."

He made a face at the fire he was still stirring. His gut was telling him that Mr. Davenport had blown into town rather suddenly — too suddenly. Something was off about the whole situation. Perhaps he should send a few telegrams to inquire into the man's background. Who was he, and what did he really want with the Byrd family?

"Allow me to clear up some of the muddle for you," he offered gently. He gave the fire one last stir before setting the poker aside. Then he turned to face her. "You are wrong about me missing you. I would miss you greatly if you left town."

She caught her lower lip between her teeth but didn't respond.

"You were right about something else, too."

Her gaze darted nervously to his.

"I wasn't demonstrating much faith when I signed that blasted mail-order bride contract. A few days ago, I sent a telegram to the agency in Savannah to cancel it, and I just this morning received confirmation that they did so."

"Why are you telling me this?" Her voice sounded a trifle breathless.

"Because that means I'm a free man, another possibility for you to consider."

The color slowly left her cheeks. "Graham," she breathed. "What exactly are you saying?"

In for a penny. Feeling like the proverbial bull in a china shop, he stumbled onward. "I'm saying that I respect your independence and would fight to protect it if you ever gave me the right to do so. I would also place myself bodily between you and anyone who ever tried to strip you of your financial assets."

She looked stunned. "That's a very kind and selfless thing to say."

"It's also true," he informed her tenderly. Advancing on her, he came to stand behind her and gently rested his hands on her shoulders. "In the short time we've known each other, I've come to the realization that there's nothing I wouldn't do for you."

She turned her head sideways, but only to squeeze her eyelids shut. "Except restore me and my family to my childhood home in Charleston."

"Except that," he admitted in a rough voice. *But that's not what you really want. We both know it.*

"What brought you to this decision?" she asked shakily.

"Heaven knows I haven't encouraged your current sentiments."

"I'm a simple man with simple tastes." He figured he'd come this far already, so he might as well continue speaking the truth. "I admire simple things like plain speaking, honesty, and hard work. In addition to those qualities, you are also beautiful, intelligent, ambitious, and loyal to those you love. Add in a sprinkling of bread flour on your fingers and the scent of biscuits in the air, and my heart never really stood a chance."

She reached up to rest her hands on his, transferring some of the flour dust to his scarred and leathery skin. "I am honored that you feel this way, Graham Christensen."

But. He sensed a but. His hands tightened on her shoulders.

"I promised to consider all the possibilities, and I am a woman of my word."

"That you are." He took a moment to breathe in the wonder of being this close to her. "It is one of the things I admire most about you."

"It also means I have two possibilities to consider, since I have two men requesting my hand in marriage. That is what you are doing, is it not?" she inquired shyly.

"I most certainly am."

"Again, I am honored." Her voice dropped to a husky near-whisper. "I also have a third option to weigh against the first two."

"What? I have another competitor?" he growled.

"Yes." He could hear the smile in her voice. "My independence."

"Which I would never take from you," he protested.

"Maybe you would not intend to, but our lives would become indelibly entwined if we wed."

"*When* we wed," he corrected with so much conviction

that he surprised even himself. "When we wed," he repeated firmly, "you will have more power at your command than you ever dreamed of, because you will own every inch of your very own blacksmith." He smiled without mirth. "It is not a claim many boarding house proprietresses can make, if any, my dearest Lilly."

A breathy sob escaped her. "Do not call me your dearest, please. Not yet."

Not yet. They were two small words, but they filled him with more hope than the entire rest of their conversation had. *Not yet* signified an event that would eventually come to pass.

"I won't call you mine again until you ask me to," he promised, "but I will continue to think of you as such, because that is what you are. Mine." It was one of the hardest things he'd ever done, but he released her shoulders and dropped his hands to his sides. "I'm taking my leave of you now — not because I want to, but because it is the only way to avoid kissing you."

He thought he heard her whisper his name again, but he couldn't be sure. He hadn't been jesting, though, about his need for air. One second longer in her presence, and he might have done something utterly regrettable, like spin her around and seal his mouth over hers.

Chapter 5: Jingle Bells

LILLY

Yours. Lilly listened to the cadence of Graham's footfalls as he left the kitchen, knowing she could no longer deny what was happening between them. There'd been something special about him from the start — something that frustrated her to no end, because she hadn't been able to shake the feeling. Graham was the kind of man who could get under a woman's skin and stay there. It was a thought that terrified her.

Already she spent far too much time thinking about him, wondering where he was and what he was up to. She also spent far too much time wondering if he was thinking about her in return. She was aware of him from the moment he walked into a room until the moment he left it, and she always felt a little bereft after he was gone — like a piece of her was missing. It was a foolish and unwise sentiment, one that threatened her hard-fought independence and equally hard-won financial security. How could she ever trust any man with such things?

If she married Graham, she would probably never be wealthy. It was unlikely they would ever return to

Charleston together to restore the war-torn plantation where she'd grown up. With him, she would never reclaim her status as a southern belle. The glory days of her childhood would remain in the past.

On the other hand, if she accepted Lee Davenport's offer, she could return home. She could take her mother and her youngest sister with her. They could walk the same flower gardens and cotton fields where her father and brothers had once labored. They would reunite with old friends and revel in rich memories.

Or Lilly could remain right where she was, as the proprietress of Rose Haven. She could reign over the tidy, well-kept building where she was currently standing until the end of her days. She could bake endless loaves of bread in this very kitchen. She could feed and shelter untold numbers of friends, loved ones, and travelers. She could give back to her community. Her many years of service would count for something. And when she reached the end of the road, she would be able to look back and know with certainty that she'd made a real difference in the world — one hungry customer at a time.

A light knock on the door frame made her jump. She spun around so quickly that her skirts slapped the table legs.

Lee Davenport was standing there, looking impeccably polite and expectant in a suit of navy silk. His black top hat was clutched in one hand, and an elegant black walking stick was clutched in the other. He leaned on it slightly as he inclined his head at her.

"A good morning to you, Miss Lilly. I trust you slept well?" His brown wavy hair was carefully slicked back from his high forehead, his sideburns neatly trimmed.

Lilly also knew that his shirt had been waxed and pressed, since she'd done the deed herself. In short, he presented the picture of a perfect southern gentleman, whereas she undoubtedly looked like a harried maid.

Glancing in dismay at her floury hands, she gave him a rueful smile. "I did, sir. I hope you enjoyed a decent night's sleep as well."

He shrugged. "I am grateful you had a bed to spare an old friend."

It wasn't a direct answer. She frowned in concern. "Do you have enough blankets? Were you warm enough?"

He shrugged again. "It's a lot colder here. No doubt you miss the southern sunshine as much as I do."

"Of course." She returned to her kneading, leaning into the dough and pushing with all of her strength. The number of visits she'd received in the kitchen this morning had put her behind schedule.

"After the fire died down, I had my memories of home to keep me warm."

She abruptly paused her kneading. "You let…" she gulped, "you mean to say, you slept in a room without a fire?" Panic flooded her mouth. *Mercy!* It was the dead of winter. It was a wonder the man was still standing and forming words. He could've been frozen into a block of ice.

He gestured with his walking stick. "My servant is staying at the livery with my driver. Alas, there was no one to tend the fire."

She stared at him in disbelief. It slowly dawned on her that she'd been removed for so long from her former life that she'd quite forgotten what it felt like to be waited on hand and foot by servants. If their roles had been reversed last night, she wouldn't have thought twice about rising from her bed, stepping into a pair of slippers, and throwing a stick of wood on her own fire. The very notion that someone else should do it for her wouldn't have even crossed her mind.

She caught her lower lip between her teeth, wondering how to solve the dilemma. She was currently the sole employee at Rose Haven. There'd been no time yet to hold interviews for expanding her staff, though Mags helped whenever she could. It certainly wouldn't be appropriate for her to enter Mr. Davenport's room in the dead of night to keep the fire going in the hearth, nor would it be any more appropriate for Mags to do so. *Good gracious!* If word got out about them tending to such a task, their reputations would be sorely compromised and tarnished beyond repair.

"I'll, ah…have someone check on your fire tonight," she promised vaguely.

"I would greatly appreciate it." Though Mr. Davenport treated her to a courtly bow, he sounded more bored than impressed.

Inwardly wincing at the thought of how cold he must have gotten last night, she pondered the list of men she could ask for help. Graham was the first name that came to mind. He would do it if she asked. However, it would be awkward to ask one of her suitors to wait on the other. No, that would never do.

Dan Forest. His apprentice's face popped into her mind next. Yes, indeed. He was the most logical solution, given her short list of options. She would ask for his aid the next time she saw him. Though his temper operated on a shorter fuse than she preferred, there was no need for any discourse between the two men. All Dan would need to do is tiptoe inside Mr. Davenport's room at midnight, stir the coals, and add a few logs to the flames. With any luck, Mr. Davenport would sleep right through it.

Mr. Davenport eyed Lilly in polite silence as she continued to work. "Is there something else that you need, sir?"

"Yes. A wife." His dark eyes twinkled at her. "I thought I made myself quite clear on the topic."

She felt her face heat. "I was referring to right this moment. You seem to be waiting for something."

"For someone," he corrected in a playful voice. "You, to be more precise."

"Me?" As kind as his attentions were, it made her a bit uncomfortable to have him in the kitchen while she was working. She eyed him curiously as she finished pounding the bread dough and set it back in the bowl to rise. Hurrying to the sink, she rinsed off her hands and arms as best as she could, knowing there was no way to remove all the flour dust from her person without taking a bath and changing outfits.

"Yes, you. I've rented a sleigh and a team of horses. I was hoping you and Mags would join me for a ride through the snow."

A sleigh ride! The romantic sound of it made her insides flutter. No one had ever asked to take her on a sleigh ride before.

"You do realize I have a boarding house to run," she informed him in as staunch of tones as she could muster in light of her weakening resistance. Oh, how she wanted to toss her responsibilities aside and join him! Just this once.

"Even hardworking proprietresses deserve a break now and then," he assured in a caressing voice.

"I want to," she sighed, "I truly do, but I wasn't jesting about my responsibilities here."

"Yes, yes." He waved a hand dismissively. "I am well aware. That is why I secured the services of Sam Bullock. He swore to me that he was capable of keeping this place running in your absence."

Relief swept through Lilly at the realization that Mr. Davenport had truly thought of everything. Sam was employed by her oldest sister, Elizabeth, and her husband, David. The elderly servant had been with David since his military days, following the drum alongside his master. The man was like family to them all.

"Then I will happily join you on your sleigh ride. Thank you for inviting me."

"My pleasure."

"How soon will Sam arrive?"

The sound of a male throat clearing behind her told her that Sam was already in the room.

She glanced over her shoulder at him. "You old dear. Are you sure you're up to baking bread and keeping my chili pots stirred?"

"Is the sky blue and the snow cold?" He gently nudged her away from the sink and started rinsing the bowls and utensils resting there.

"It's more gray than blue today but very, very cold."

"Close enough." He angled his head at the door. "Scoot. I work best when I'm alone."

"I'm scooting." She beamed another smile at him. "Do make yourself at home and sample anything you wish."

As he continued scrubbing, she dashed from the room to change and nearly collided with Graham.

"Oh! It's you again." Her feet churned to a halt in the dimly lit hallway.

His green gaze seemed to drink her in. "I know I said I'd keep my distance, but I just finished working on these." He held out a pair of new long-handled soup ladles. "I overheard you fretting about how short the handles on your other ones were, so I figured this was the best remedy."

"Graham!" She accepted his gifts, marveling at how sturdy and well-made they were. He'd even etched a pattern of trailing vines around the handles. "They are exactly what I need. How can I ever thank you?" There would be no more dropping her serving spoons inside her stewpots. These were long enough to rest against the rim without falling in.

"Well, I was wondering if you'd be willing to take a walk with me." He glanced bashfully away from her. "Though I've no desire to rush your decision about my proposal, I also have no desire to spend long periods of time away from you. The truth is, the moment I left your kitchen an hour ago, I started missing you."

The raw emotion in his voice tugged at her senses. As disconcerting as the discovery was, she'd missed him, too. "I would love to take a walk with you, Graham, but—"

"No buts." His gaze lit with joy. "We've already spent too long dancing around the what ifs. I'll go fetch your coat from the hall tree."

"I can't." Her heart constricted, knowing what she was about to say would be hard for him to hear. "A few minutes ago, I agreed to attend a sleigh ride with Mr. Davenport and my youngest sister. I am heading to change right now."

"Change?" He scowled at her. "What for?"

She raised and lowered her shoulders. "To go riding."

"You are beautiful just as you are."

She blushed deeply. "I am drenched in flour, and my hands smell like chopped celery and carrots."

"As I mentioned before, I very much like seeing you this way, Miss Byrd. Anyone who doesn't appreciate such a delightful view is the world's biggest fool."

"You sound jealous." She attempted to brush past him.

"I *am* jealous." He stepped directly in her path, tipping her chin up with one finger and forcing her gaze to meet his. "I am also surprised."

"At what?" She swatted his hand away from her chin.

"At the very idea you'd consider giving up your many dreams and goals to become dependent on a man like Mr. Davenport."

"On the contrary, I don't wish to be dependent on any man," she snapped.

"If you give up Rose Haven and move back to Charleston, you'll be dependent on him for every coin in your reticule, every bite of food you take," he warned.

"Oh, give way!" She pushed her way around him at last. "This conversation isn't about me. It never was. It's about you and your desire to have me dependent on you instead of any other man."

"You're wrong," he called after her. His voice echoed off the hardwood floor and tin ceiling tiles. "All I want is your happiness, Lilly Byrd."

"And you believe you're the man to make that happen, eh?" Her heart was racing so hard that she had to press a hand over the organ to steady it as she reached the door of her suite.

"I am the only man who can," he returned with quiet conviction. "Mark my words, it's all you'll be thinking about during your upcoming sleigh ride with that insufferable windbag."

A breathy laugh escaped her as she listened to Graham's retreating footsteps. When she allowed herself a peek down the hallway, she caught him glancing back at her. However, he didn't stop walking away.

"Graham Christensen," she whispered as she twisted her doorknob and stepped inside her room. "What am I going to do with you?"

He was right about one thing, though; he was all she could think about. In fact, she'd been so busy thinking about him that she'd carried her new soup ladles all the way to her bed chamber. With a sigh, she laid them on the bench at the foot of her bed. She would take them to the kitchen on her next trip there.

While she studied the gowns in her wardrobe, it dawned on her that Graham had never before seen her in anything but her work dresses — plain gray and plain brown, black lace-up boots, and an apron or two. What would he think of her if she donned one of the lacy gowns of her past? He'd declared he was a simple man with simple tastes. Would he find her ball gowns too fussy and pretentious?

She'd watched his apprentice curl his lip more than once at Mags' many delightful creations with needle and thread. It hurt Lilly's heart a little at the way the hotheaded young blacksmith in training seemed to have no appreciation for her sister's gift. It didn't prevent him from following her around with his gaze, however. Maybe someday Mags would win him over.

With a sigh, Lilly finally settled on a gown of green wool. She tried to tell herself that it reminded her of spruces and evergreens. That was only partly true, however. It also reminded her of Graham's adoring gaze. It might be a bit fussy for his tastes, but he would like her in this gown. She was sure of it.

She twisted her blonde hair up next and added a pair of pearl earrings her mother had given her years ago. They added a soft and feminine touch to her outfit that always made her feel like a real lady. As she gave a twirl in front of the mirror, her mind drifted back to the old days when she'd dressed like this every day.

This was the life Mr. Lee Davenport was offering her. It was so kind and generous of him that she wished she could remember more about him and his family. Guilt shivered through her at the realization she could not. His father had owned a set of warehouses down by the docks. The Davenports hadn't come from old family money like hers. They were a shipping family with newly acquired wealth, all of which had come from trade.

Their families had not attended the same parties or moved in the same circles. She and Lee Davenport had not even attended the same schools. He'd certainly not shared her private tutors, music instructors, or dance coaches. Back then, they might as well have come from different worlds. It was the same today, with one monumental difference — somewhere along the way, they'd swapped worlds.

Shaking her head at the odd turns that her life had taken, Lilly stepped from her room and glided down the hallway. She paused at the sound of angry voices coming from the private sitting room in the back of the boarding house.

Her heart sank as she recognized first Mags' voice and then that of Dan Forest. *Oh, dear!* It sounded like the two of them were flying at each other like alley cats. She debated stepping into the room to play the part of a peacemaker. However, she hesitated, knowing it was something they were eventually going to have to work out between them. No one could do it for them.

"He's a snob!" Dan sounded furiously indignant. "How can you not see that?"

"Well, you are rude and crass. How is that any better?"

"At least, I'm honest."

"About hating me. I am well aware," she fumed.

"I do not hate you."

"Is that why you're always insulting me and looking down your nose at me?" she shot back.

"That shoe is on the other foot, and you know it." His voice grew cold. "You disapproved of me the moment we met. You're forever turning up your nose at my shirts and trousers—"

"Because they are atrocious!" she cut in. "If you weren't so stubborn, you'd hand them over to me like I've asked repeatedly. I could fix them in two snaps."

"I don't need you filling my garments with fancy stitches. They are good enough as they are."

"Good is not an adjective any sane person would use to describe shirts and trousers so threadbare that you could freeze to death in them."

"See? That's what I'm talking about. You're as much of a snob as that stuffed shirt you're about to go driving with."

"I am not!"

"Then prove it."

"I am under no obligation to prove anything to an ill-mannered boor like yourself."

"You know what? You deserve each other," he sneered. "I reckon I'll be hearing about your pending nuptials soon."

"You have no idea what you're talking about, Dan Forest. If you did, you wouldn't be spouting such nonsense."

"So you're not marrying the cad?" he demanded sarcastically.

"Oh, give way!" she fumed. "I am going on a sleigh ride with a beloved sister and a friend from Charleston. That is all."

"A friend who's made it very clear he wants to marry you."

"If I wanted to avoid every man who wishes to marry me, I would have to leave Cowboy Creek, something I have no plan of doing anytime soon."

"Well, I'll be!" His voice changed to one of marvel. "You really don't mean to marry the cad."

"You're the only fool who ever thought I did," she assured crisply.

"Then why are you going driving with him at all?"

"Finally a sensible question. I didn't know you were capable of such a thing."

"There you go again," he sighed.

"Fine. If you insist on knowing, I intend to chaperone my sister. I'm also going to enjoy the sleigh ride, whether you think I have the right to or not, you iron-hearted black-smith. This southern gal loves the snow, and Mr. Lee Davenport happens to be the first and only man this season who's offered to take me out in it." With those words, she stormed from the room.

Though her startled glance landed on Lilly in the hall-way, she kept walking. Lilly was fairly certain her sister's eyes were damp. However, it wasn't the best time to go after her. Now might be the only chance Lilly had to secure Dan's help for the evening.

Drawing a deep breath, she entered the parlor.

Dan, who'd been standing by the hearth with his head resting on his arm, abruptly straightened. "If you've come back to tear into me some more—" His voice died at the sight of Lilly. Looking shamefaced, he nodded a greeting at her.

"Actually, I came to ask a favor," she informed him softly.

"What do you need?" He frowned in concern.

"It's about our stuffed shirt guest, Mr. Lee Davenport."

Dan's neck turned red. "I reckon you overheard our conversation."

"Parts of it." She smiled sadly at him. "I am sorry things have been so difficult between you and my sister."

He glanced away. "I'm the one who's mucked it up."

"Well, what I have to ask of you might help."

He eagerly turned back to her.

"Mr. Davenport is accustomed to being waited on by servants, even in the middle of the night. Alas, Mags and I are the only ones here at the boarding house to tend to the needs of our guests."

Dan balled his fists at his sides. "By all that is holy! What in tarnation does he need tended in the middle of the night?" He looked angry enough to do harm.

"His fire. He let it die in the hearth last night and nearly suffered his death of cold."

Dan's brows shot up. "Surely you jest."

"I wish I was jesting."

"Let the nincompoop freeze, then."

"He's an old friend, as well as my guest," she reminded. "I was hoping you would be kind enough to pay his room a visit around midnight and add a few logs to the fire."

"How will this help me mend fences with Magnolia?"

"You're just going to have to trust me on this one, Dan."

He shook his head. "I can't believe I'm agreeing to this."

"I can." She surprised them both by gliding across the room and standing on her tiptoes to kiss his cheek. "You're a good man, Dan Forest."

"You're sister doesn't think so."

"Yes, she does." Lilly stepped back. "Just be patient with her."

"I'm not a very patient man," he confessed.

"If you truly care about her, you will scrape up a little of it." She reached out to squeeze the top of his arm. Then she turned and left the room.

Mags and their mother were already tucked inside the rear seat of the sleigh when Lilly stepped outside. A team of reddish-brown horses were stamping the ground, impatient to be off. Each stomp of their hooves made the bells jingle that were tied to their lines.

Lee Davenport glanced up from tending the horses to give Lilly an admiring once-over. "You made it at last." As he lifted her into the front seat of the sleigh, he seemed reluctant to let her hand go.

Lilly swallowed a sigh, knowing that anyone who was watching them wouldn't fail to miss his preferential treatment. By their seating arrangement alone, he was declaring his intentions to pursue her over her sister.

She could only hope that Graham Christensen wasn't one of the many townsfolk who was watching them drive away.

Chapter 6: Fiery Mishap

GRAHAM

Mid December

Graham tried to ignore the many rumors flying around about Lilly Byrd and Lee Davenport in the days following their sleigh ride. It wasn't easy, though. They were the talk of the town. He doubted many dapper fellows from the Old South had ever graced the streets of Cowboy Creek with their presence like Mr. Davenport was doing. He carried himself like a duke who owned the world, spending lavish amounts of money on gifts for the Byrds. Every time Graham saw him promenading down one sidewalk or another with his ridiculous walking stick, he had to look the other way.

What do you see in him, Lilly? Graham couldn't understand the man's appeal — not on any level. From his perspective, Lee Davenport was weak, idle, and lazy. The only thing the man had going for him was his wealth.

Rolling to his side after another sleepless night, he stared at the blackened window, watching the first glow rise on the horizon.

"Put a sock in it, will you?" Dan groaned from the other side of the bed.

"Huh?" Though his thoughts had been jogging a mile per minute the entire night, Graham wasn't aware he'd said anything aloud.

"How's a man supposed to sleep through such loud moping and pining over there?"

"I don't know what you're talking about," Graham retorted stiffly.

"Just admit it. You're in love with her."

Graham closed his eyes. "Is it that obvious?"

"To me? Yes. To her? I have no idea."

"I asked her to marry me," he confessed.

"Whoa!" Dan shot to a sitting position in bed, throwing back the quilts. "When did this happen?"

"A few days ago."

"And she turned you down flat," Dan sighed. "That figures."

"Actually, she didn't." Graham sat up with a weary huff, feeling the weight of the world on his shoulders. He hadn't slept much in over a week.

"Doesn't sound like she said yes, either."

"That is correct. She promised to consider my offer right alongside Davenport's."

Dan snorted in derision as he swung his legs over his side of the bed. "There is no way she's going to chain herself to such a nauseating bloke as him. She's too smart for that. My vote is that you'll win in the end, boss."

"Will I?" Graham ran a weary hand over his scruffy jaw. "She's a very independent-minded woman. I'm not convinced she wants to marry any of us."

"Then we'll just have to work harder to convince her." Dan started to whistle as he tugged on his shirt and boots.

"You're mighty cheerful today," Graham grumbled.

"You say that like it's a rare thing," his apprentice retorted. "I'm always cheerful."

Graham stood and stretched. "You do realize where all liars are going, right?"

"Well, that's a fine thought to start the morning on." Dan zinged a pillow in his direction.

Graham caught it, tossed it back, and missed.

Dan shook his head. "That's just pitiful. So pitiful, in fact, that I'm going to head on down the street to fire up the forge alone. I'd like to get an early start on the set of wagon wheels I promised that rancher in the next county over. I'll meet you back here for breakfast in about an hour."

Graham nodded glumly as he glanced toward their dying fire in the hearth. It was time to bank the coals. Though everything looked alright from where he stood beside the bed, it seemed to him that there was more smoke in the room than usual. It might not hurt to check out the flue before tonight to ensure there was no blockage.

Dan gave a tentative sniff. "You smell that smoke, boss?"

"I never stop smelling it." Graham rolled his shoulders to work out a kink. "It's one of the joys of being a blacksmith."

"I agree, but this is different. It smells like something is wrong." Dan scowled as he sniffed the air again.

The two men glanced at each other as it dawned on them that the extra smoke filling their room wasn't coming from the fireplace against the wall.

"Fire!" they cried in unison.

"Come on!" Graham shouted. Yanking his shirt from the bedpost, he shrugged it on while stepping into his boots.

Dan had already flung open the door of their room.

Graham dashed after him, still buttoning his shirt.

The hallways of the boarding house were in pandemonium. Guests were flapping about in their night robes, hollering back and forth and trying to figure out what was wrong.

A muffled scream made Graham head straight for the kitchen. There he found Lilly on a step-stool, wrestling with the damper over her stove.

"Here. Let me." Without waiting for her permission, he lifted her down to fiddle with it himself. In seconds, he concluded what was amiss. The damper was jammed closed. No, it was worse than that. The knob had broken off entirely.

"It's just smoke," he announced as Dan careened into the room. "Damper's broken. We need to get as many windows and doors open as we can."

In minutes, they had the place well ventilated, which most unfortunately meant the icy winter gale outside was whistling through their midst.

Lee Davenport staggered into the kitchen, well after the crisis was in hand. "Jimminies!" he grumbled. "What is the meaning of this?"

"It's a broken damper," Graham explained, trying not to grin at the fellow's ruffled shirt and silk night robe. *Good gravy!* He wouldn't have been caught dead in such a ridiculous get-up. "No need to worry. I'll have it fixed in no time." As far as he could tell, nothing more than a new knob would need to be welded on. He'd already sent Dan down the street to fetch their stump forge and a few other tools.

"Brr!" Mr. Davenport shivered and clutched his robe more tightly around him. "I'll go on and get dressed for the day, so I can oversee the repairs."

Oversee? Graham stared at the man, sorely doubting he

knew the first thing about the mechanics of a cooking stove.

"Nonsense!" Lilly assured hastily after a glance at Graham. "There's no need to trouble yourself over something so trifling, sir. Besides, you'll be much warmer in your room. It's as cold as the Arctic in here."

The man shivered delicately again, and it was all Graham could do not to snicker.

"I trust your fire was to your liking the last few nights," she continued.

Mr. Davenport smirked. "Other than having a servant who clatters around like a bull at a stampede, yes. I am much warmer with a fire that lasts until morning."

Dan returned to the kitchen, lugging the stump forge he'd retrieved from the shop. "Here you go, boss." The irritated glance he flicked in Mr. Davenport's direction told Graham that he'd overheard the man's complaining.

Dan waited until both Lilly and Mr. Davenport left the room before exclaiming, "A bull on a stampede? That's an exaggeration of sinful proportions. I feel like I'm tiptoeing through the tulips every time I step into his blasted presence."

Graham grimaced as they arranged the stump forge next to the hearth in the kitchen. "I take it he's had the misfortune to wake up while you were in the room?"

"Every night." Dan couldn't have sounded more disgusted. "He usually insists I run and fetch a cup of tea or empty his chamber pot." He wrinkled his nose in disgust. "You do not want to know how many times I've been sorely tempted to dump the contents of it in his sneering face, but I do not wish to create any trouble for Lilly."

"I heard my name." Lilly returned to the room with a pile of blankets in her arms. "Pray assure me that my two

favorite blacksmiths were saying nice things about me."
She smiled tiredly at them over the top of her stack.

Graham hurried forward to relieve her of the burden.
He set the pile of blankets on the end of her preparation
counter. "What's all this for?"

"To cover the windows. It's miserably cold in here."

Her kindness was touching. "You needn't go to such
trouble on our account, though we appreciate the thought.
We'll have your damper fixed shortly." Without thinking,
he reached out to run a finger down her cheek.

She went still beneath his touch. "Thank you," she said
softly.

"For what?"

"For rolling out of bed in the wee hours of the
morning to come to my rescue." She muffled a yawn.

"It's no trouble." He resisted the urge to tuck a stray
lock of hair behind her ear. "I'm a blacksmith. We're
always up early."

She made a face. "So am I."

"Maybe you should go back to bed," he muttered.
"You look tired."

Her blue eyes widened. "I have breakfast to prepare
and a boarding house to run, in case you've forgotten."

"I have not. However, I doubt it would be difficult for
you to rustle up some extra help, if you'd like to get a little
more sleep."

She slapped her hands down on her hips. "I could, but
I won't. I'll get my second wind soon. You, on the other
hand, look more tired than I do. Is something wrong with
your bed?"

"No."

"Or your pillow?"

"It's fine, lass."

"Do you have enough blankets?"

"I said I'm fine."

"You don't look fine."

"He's not." Dan chucked Graham's shoulder as he sauntered past. "He's pining away night after night for his heart's desire."

Her face blossomed such a brilliant shade of pink that Graham wanted to throttle his apprentice.

Dan spared him an unholy grin. "If you'll excuse me, boss, I'm heading to the roof to check out the chimney while you stay down here and…" he smirked knowingly, "handle the repair."

"Is it true?" Lilly whispered after Dan left the room, whistling maddeningly again.

"Does it matter?" he countered. To avoid meeting her gaze, he used his tongs to lift the iron pellet he intended to use for the next damper knob. Carrying it to the hearth, he thrust it into the open flames.

"It does to me." She moved to stand beside him.

"I'm still waiting for your answer to my suit," he reminded in undertones.

"And I'm still praying for the Lord's guidance on the matter."

"I want a wife and a family of my own, Lilly. I want it more than I've ever wanted anything else."

"You have no family left at all?" Her voice was hesitant.

It wasn't a topic he enjoyed discussing. "My parents passed during my early teens. I've been on my own ever since."

"How sad! I am sorry to hear it."

"I survived."

"You more than survived," she said warmly. "You're a skilled craftsman and business owner. Those things do not happen by accident."

"You are correct. It took a five-year apprenticeship."

He didn't bother telling her about the many hardships along the way, about how he'd slept on the hearth for the first two years of his apprenticeship since he had no place else to go. No family and no home — two things he was determined to have soon.

"I can only imagine the stories you have to tell, Graham."

He smiled. "That I do."

"If we ever get around to going on that walk we talked about, you can tell me a few of them."

His breathing turned rough. Was the woman of his dreams finally giving him permission to court her?

"That is, if you still have any interest in a jaunt through the snow with me," she added uncertainly.

"You know that I do." He wanted to stroll hand in hand through the vast whiteness of his first northern Texas winter with her. He didn't care what direction they went, so long as they were together.

"Then name a time," she ordered breathlessly. "We'll never stop being busy, you and I. We'll simply have to steal the time together and go."

Steal the time together. He liked her choice of words and the wistfulness behind them. "I love you, Lilly." It wasn't something he'd planned to say this soon, but the timing felt right.

She caught her breath sharply. After a pause, she swallowed hard. "You do?" she squeaked.

"Very much." The way he felt about her wasn't simply a passing fancy. It was real, and it was lasting. "Is there a chance you'll ever return my feelings?" He slowly spun the iron pellet in the flames.

"Yes. I believe there is."

It was a cryptic answer that didn't tell him much more than he already knew.

"What is holding you back?" He cast a longing sideways glance at her.

"Fear," she confessed in a tremulous voice.

He was shocked to see a tear roll down her cheek. The dampness mingled with the soot settling from the air and left a muddy trail.

"You're afraid of me?" Her words couldn't have stunned him more.

"Not of you, but of the future. Of making a mistake." The tremble in her voice grew more pronounced. "Marriage is a forever kind of decision, Graham. It is something I would prefer to get right the first time around."

"Me, too." He wanted to kiss her so badly that he had to force himself to take a step away from her. He had the perfect excuse, since the iron pellet was now glowing red and gold. Moving across the room, he transferred the pellet to his forge and reached for his hammer.

There was something remarkably intimate about swinging his hammer in the presence of the woman he loved. He could feel her eyes on him as he pounded the pellet into shape, one ringing strike at a time. There was a cadence to his work that never grew old. Watching the finished product take shape filled him with immense satisfaction.

Once the new knob was properly formed, he thrust it back in the fire to heat it again. Only after it was glowing red again did he carry it to the flue. He gave the knob several light taps to settle the melted end into place. Then he continued to hold it while it hardened and cooled.

Now was probably the time to let her know how dangerous old pipes could be. "Not to scare you, Lilly, but the jammed damper could've resulted in a house fire. We were fortunate this time around."

Alarm swept her delicate features. "What are you saying, Graham?"

"As a precaution, Dan and I should probably do a thorough exam of every wood-burning stove and fireplace in the building."

"Oh, dear!" she sighed. "That sounds like a tremendous amount of work."

"You'll sleep better at night after we do so."

"Very well, Graham. I'll allow it so long as you let me pay you for your time."

"I reckon we could work something out." He had no intention of taking her money, though. Maybe she could make him a pie or cobbler. He didn't want their relationship to deteriorate into something as mundane as a series of paid transactions, which was exactly what was going to happen soon if he didn't step up his efforts to win her heart.

He rubbed a hand over his jaw as a plan of action formed in his mind. Perhaps he was being hasty and jumping to all the wrong conclusions about Mr. Davenport, but he first wanted to determine if the man was a worthy competitor. All it would take was a visit to the telegraph office to send an inquiry to a few friends in the south.

Specifically, he wanted to know if Mr. Lee Davenport was everything he claimed to be — a wealthy gentleman and homeowner. More specifically, was he truly in possession of the Byrds' former family estate? Try as he might, Graham couldn't shake the feeling that there was something undeniably odd about the fellow showing up out of the blue like this in pursuit of a wife. Why now? Where had the man been for the last two years while the Byrd family spiraled towards poverty?

"You seem quiet all of a sudden," Lilly mused. "Are you regretting your offer to inspect this old building?"

"Not at all. I was just thinking."

"About?"

There was no way he could relate his concerns about Mr. Davenport to her without sounding like a jealous suitor, so he settled for a partial truth. "About how I'd better help you get these windows closed and the room cleaned up before heading back to my shop." He reached for the first window sash.

"No way are you staying to clean my kitchen, Graham. You've done enough already." Lilly reached for a basket and filled it with bread, butter, and preserves. "Take this to share with Dan. Something tells me once the two of you get to work, you'll not return for breakfast."

"You know me well."

"I'm trying to." She tipped her head back to smile up at him.

"This means you care about me, too." He tapped the handle of the basket.

Her blue gaze softened. "Of course I do." She shooed him from the room. "Now get on with you. Sometimes a woman simply needs to be alone in her kitchen."

Especially one as independent as she. "I can take a hint." He winked at her.

"You understand me fairly well, too," she sighed.

He nodded, caressing her with his eyes. Getting to know her better was both his highest priority and his greatest joy lately. "I'll send Dan back later to get the forge out of your way."

"No hurry. I don't mind working around it."

He wanted to say more, but he didn't want her to feel like he was needlessly hovering.

On his way back to his shop, he took a detour to the

telegraph office to dictate a few telegrams to the clerk there. He addressed the first one to the sheriff in Savannah. The second one went to a blacksmith friend in Charleston. Graham was anxious to hear what both men had to say about the aristocratic visitor in Cowboy Creek.

He moseyed on down the street to the door of his shop. Before he could turn the handle, however, he was arrested by the sound of a woman's voice on the other side.

He paused to listen.

"You ripped your shirt on your way down from the roof," Magnolia Byrd accused.

"Why do you care?" There was a clattering sound as if Dan was puttering with his tools.

"Because you and Graham may very well have prevented Rose Haven from burning down this morning. I am grateful to you both."

"You're welcome. Can we talk about something else?"

"No."

Graham moved to the window to peek inside.

Magnolia had her hand out. "Take your shirt off. Now!"

Dan gave her an incredulous look. "I hardly think that's appropriate."

"I don't care. Your shirt is in desperate need of mending." She kept her hand outstretched.

"I'll take care of it myself." He curled his lip at her. "I've told you again and again that I can't afford such luxuries."

"Good gracious, Dan! You're the stubbornest man I've ever run across. I simply want to mend your ratty shirt."

"And I'm going to pass on your offer."

"Then you leave me no choice," she snapped.

"No choice for what?"

"For what I'm about to do." She stormed out the front

door of the shop, not seeming to notice that Graham was standing a mere few feet away. She jogged to her seamstress shop and returned, clutching a package in her arms.

"Here." She tossed it at Dan the moment she stepped back inside.

He caught it. "What's this?" he asked suspiciously.

"A new shirt, since you continually refuse to let me repair your old one."

He looked flabbergasted. "You made me a new shirt?"

"Oh, dear! Is something wrong with your hearing now?"

"I cannot accept it. I've told you again and again I'm not some dandified buffoon who requires such luxuries." He tried to hand the shirt back to her, but she danced out of his reach.

"Oh, for crying out loud! Just put on the dratted thing and hush."

He looked confused. "Why are you doing this?"

She rolled her eyes heavenward. "Lord, forgive the man. He wouldn't recognize an olive branch if it slapped him between the eyeballs."

"You're saying you want to be allies?"

She gave a long-suffering sigh. "Well, I'm beyond weary of being enemies. Arguing with you is like wrestling with a donkey. All you feel is exhausted afterward."

His lips twitched. "If we call a truce, will I be required to give you a gift in return?"

She pinched her thumb and forefinger together and held them beneath his nose. "I am this close to slapping you right now."

He snickered. "At least I'm being honest. You may as well know up front that I don't have the coin to shower you with expensive gifts like your nauseating beau from Charleston."

"It doesn't require money to pick a wildflower now and then, you knot head."

His smirk deepened. "I'm a blacksmith, Magnolia. Not a daisy picker."

"It doesn't cost anything to be kind, either. You should try it sometime."

While he stood there looking confused, she stormed out of the shop a second time. "He's all yours," she snarled at Graham. "I've had enough of him for one day."

He stepped inside and slowly closed the door behind him. "Well, well, well. You and Magnolia Byrd, eh?"

"Don't start in on me." Dan stared in dismay at the shirt he was turning over in his hands. "My brain is still too raw from dealing with that woman."

"Are you going to try on the shirt?" Graham turned aside to fiddle with their collection of tongs in order to hide a smile.

"I reckon I don't have much choice," Dan sighed. "I can't bear the thought of listening to any more of her caterwauling on the subject."

"True. Very true." Graham turned around to face his friend, no longer trying to hide his mirth. "Do you want to know what else won't cost any money after the two of you start courting?"

Dan shook his head. "Exactly how much of our conversation did you overhear?"

"Enough." Graham chuckled.

His apprentice blew out a long, weary breath. "By all means, then, enlighten me. What else can I do for that troublesome wench that won't cost me an arm and a leg?"

"You could kiss her."

Chapter 7: Christmas Deadline

LILLY

Two weeks before Christmas, Mr. Lee Davenport hired a courier to deliver invitations for a holiday dinner and musicale at the home of Mr. and Mrs. Charley and Grace Arrington. As it turned out, only the Byrds and their closest friends received invitations.

Lilly left hers on the kitchen cabinet all afternoon just so she could scowl at it. As hoped for, Sam stopped by for dinner. As soon as she served the last slice of apple pie to her guests, she begged his assistance at the front desk.

He scratched his chin and pretended to consider her request. "I reckon I could stay a spell if you can rustle up another piece of that pie."

"I'll package it and send it home with you," she promised.

"Then you have yourself a deal."

She hurriedly donned her coat and hat, then headed to the livery to saddle up a horse. She had a few choice things to say to her older sister.

Grace was standing vigil by the gathering room

window which overlooked the front lawn as Lilly rode up the driveway.

She threw open the front door of the massive stone mansion before Lilly had the chance to knock.

"What were you thinking?" Lilly demanded, stepping inside the vast, two-story entry foyer. A candelabra flickered with light from a credenza, making shadows dance against the dark wood paneling.

"I did it for you, sweetie." Grace held out both arms to her sister. "A part of me knew it would bring you running even sooner. How I've missed you!"

"I do not have time for parties these days." Lilly did feel guilty, though, about how long it had been since their last sisterly visit.

"Then make time," Grace said firmly. "It's nearly Christmas." Linking her arm with Lilly's, she glided with her into the front parlor. Her rose-colored gown swished delightfully with each step. Lilly had no doubt the frothy ensemble was one of their youngest sister's creations. "Though I'm as happy as I can be about Martha Gable's decision to hand you the keys to Rose Haven, I have greatly missed you ever since."

"Missed me! I'm not that far away." The roads ran in both directions, for crying out loud!

"Yes. I've missed you." Grace nudged her toward the pianoforte on the side of the room. "When you lived in the carriage house out back, I saw a lot more of you."

"You can visit Rose Haven any time for a meal, you know. Mags comes all the time." Lilly allowed her sister to wave her onto the stool behind the pianoforte.

"Maybe I will, but it won't be the same," Grace sighed.

"What do you mean?" Lilly ran her hands lovingly over the keys of the beautiful instrument, going through the motions of playing without coaxing any sound from it just yet.

"You work from dawn until dusk. If I stop by, I worry you'll be bustling around the room, serving half the town and not paying a lick of attention to me."

"I'm paying attention to you now." Lilly ducked her head guiltily, knowing her sister's words were true. It had never been her intention, but her new duties at the boarding house had caused her to neglect her family for months.

"Only because you rode here to fuss at me about the party." Grace held up a finger when Lilly started to splutter. "Wait. I'm not finished saying my piece. I know you've always preferred to do things your way, but a boarding house is too much work for one person. You need more time to be young, my dear. To attend social gatherings and to court young men."

Here comes the sisterly scolding. "That's what this is really about, isn't it?" Lilly raised her chin. Apparently, a delightful side effect of being busy meant her sisters were having a harder time pulling off their matchmaking shenanigans. "You're worried that you and Charley are going to be stuck looking after your homely spinster sister for the rest of your days."

"You are not the least bit homely!" Grace gasped. "It's true I'm not overly enamored with your style of gowns these days, but those workaday browns and grays do not diminish your loveliness one bit."

"Thank you." A burst of wickedness propelled Lilly to add, "Then again, any insults to my face and form would reflect right back on you, since we look enough alike to pass as twins."

"Do not try to sidetrack me from the topic at hand,"

her sister admonished severely. "I'm not finished with your scolding."

Lilly mockingly inclined her head. "I can't believe I rode this far for a tongue lashing."

"Grin and bear it, my dear, because you need to hear what I am about to say next. In short, you cannot continue to run the boarding house alone. Don't bother arguing the point, because it only took one look at you to see how bone-weary you are."

Lilly grimaced, unable to deny she was exhausted.

"You need to hire more help before it drains you from the inside-out."

"It's not that simple. There are reasons I like doing things my way, and it's not just stubbornness." Lilly couldn't bear the thought of turning her kitchen over to anyone else. "It's to ensure things get done correctly. I have a lot of folks depending on me these days."

"Then train an assistant to do things your way." Grace gave a decided nod. "Pray recall that Widow Gable didn't run the place alone, either. She had you."

Lilly made a rueful face. "I know you're right, but—"

"Of course I'm right! Have I taught you nothing? Older sisters are always right."

"They like to think they are, at any rate," Lilly grumbled.

"How about we quit worrying about who's right and simply get that advertisement posted for some help at the boarding house?"

"I suppose I could add it to my list of things to do." Lilly didn't know when she'd find the time to make the poster or hold the interviews, but she'd figure it out.

"Or you could let me create the announcement for you. I dare say, my penmanship is the finest of all our sisters."

Lilly pursed her lips. "I hate asking you to go to that kind of trouble on my behalf."

Grace threw her hands in the air. "See? That's exactly what I'm talking about. Learn to delegate, little sister. It'll save you hours of time and energy. Here, I'll show you how it's done. Pretend I'm you." She struck a pose over the pianoforte with her hands clasped under her chin. "Yes, Grace, darling. I would adore your assistance with my sign. Your handwriting is absolutely lovely."

Lilly snorted. "How about we just pretend I already said it?"

"Good. I look forward to making your sign. Now play me a tune before you go." Grace waved at the piano.

"I will," Lilly held her sister's snapping blue gaze a moment longer, "right after you explain to me why you agreed to let Mr. Lee Davenport commandeer your home for a holiday party I didn't ask for."

"Because you're my sister, and I love you."

"Neither of which are reasons to hold a party."

"They most certainly are, if the gentleman in question is planning to go down on one knee and propose marriage to her."

Lilly's mouth fell open. "You have no way of knowing that."

"Oh, but I do, dearest. Call it intuition or whatever you want. Sometimes big sisters just know things."

"Did Mr. Davenport drop any hints in that direction?"

"Mercy, yes! He couldn't stop singing your praises the entire time we were visiting. He's really taken with you."

Lilly had no answer for that. Instead, she ran her fingers over the keys, this time filling the room with Christmas music.

Grace listened for several minutes. When Lilly paused

at the end of the song, she murmured, "I am going to miss you unbearably when you return to Charleston."

Lilly abruptly lifted her hands from the keyboard. "Who says I'm going to Charleston?"

Grace's blue eyes widened innocently. "Well, if you accept Lee's offer…"

"He hasn't even proposed yet," Lilly snapped.

"But he is going to, sister dear. You'd best prepare yourself."

Lilly trilled two high notes on the pianoforte. "He just arrived in town. As you've so bluntly pointed out, I've been busy working my fingers to a nubbin. We haven't had the opportunity to spend much time together."

"Except when he took you on that sleigh ride," Grace pointed out slyly.

"We were not alone, even then. Both Mother and Mags were in attendance."

Grace ignored her words. "It was the talk of the town for days. Folks were ready to start placing bets on which sister he planned to wed."

Lilly rolled her eyes. "Do you remember much about him? From Charleston, that is."

Grace shook her head, sobering. "No. Do you?"

"Very little, other than the fact his family was involved in shipping." Davenport Shipping, if she correctly recalled the name of his family's business. It was interesting how Mr. Davenport had not once spoken about it to her. He seemed far more interested in what was happening inside his family's stables. His sole passion, as far as she could tell, was horses. Or horse racing, to be more precise.

"Ah, yes! The taint of trade money." Grace's voice was sarcastic. "Do you remember when we thought such foolish things mattered?"

"Sadly, I do." Lilly lightly played through the notes on

the C major scale. "I remember when last names mattered, too, along with the cut of one's ball gown."

"And the name of one's seamstress," her sister added. "Good heavens, but we were a petty, frivolous gaggle of ladies back then!"

"Those were different times." Lilly moved her hands to the key of D and played another scale.

"Do you miss Charleston?" her sister asked wistfully.

"Sometimes. Not the pomp of high society, though." She was far more suited to the simple country life in Cowboy Creek. It was uncomplicated and peaceful.

"Me, either."

"I miss Father."

"Yes," Grace whispered.

"And our brothers."

"So very much."

When Lilly raised her gaze, she found her sister's eyes had grown damp. "Returning to Charleston won't bring them back."

"No."

"Do you think it would give mother any comfort to return to our home there? To our memories? Or would it only make her sad?" Lilly couldn't bear the thought of reliving the triple tragedy they'd suffered during the war.

Grace shook her head helplessly. "I truly do not know. You should ask Mother what she wants."

"I tried, but she seems determined not to influence my decision one way or the other."

Grace nodded. "She has always been like that, accepting whatever comes her way with the grace of a true lady."

"What about you? Do you think I should marry Mr. Davenport?" One big downside of restoring her mother to her former home was the fact that a move back to Charleston would split their family up again.

Grace gave a short chuckle. "If you do, you'll have to start using his given name."

Lilly groaned at the ceiling. "Yet another Byrd female who refuses to give me a straight answer."

"Because it is a decision only you can make, sweetie. Search your heart, and talk to the Lord about it."

For some reason, her sister's words made her think of Graham. He, too, relied on his faith for his biggest decisions. Bless his heart! He'd even gone and cancelled his mail-order bride contract. She truly hoped he was following the Lord's guidance on the matter, not merely allowing his feelings for her to cloud his judgment. He was a good man. That she didn't doubt. And she wanted so badly to believe that his declarations of love were the forever kind. Not too long ago, however, he'd been willing to marry the first woman the bridal agency sent his way. She needed time to make sure his change of heart in her direction was permanent — time that Mr. Davenport didn't seem inclined to give her. Lilly was very much afraid she was going to be forced to make some very difficult decisions soon. Sooner than she was ready.

"And now for the topic you've been avoiding." Without any further preamble, Grace changed the subject. "What's this I hear about the new blacksmith spending the winter at Rose Haven?"

Lilly stopped playing the pianoforte, drawing a bracing breath. "He and his apprentice are my newest boarders. There was a mix-up with his mail-order bride. She got misrouted and wed to someone else, I believe. Then the poor man's construction company notified him that his cabin would not be move-in ready before spring. He is most fortunate I had a vacancy."

Grace nodded thoughtfully. "Charley was surprised they weren't staying at the loft over the livery. He said two young bachelors like them could've gotten in real cheap."

"I advised Mr. Christensen of that very thing on our first meeting. However, he made it clear he prefers the peace and privacy of Rose Haven over a bunkhouse of rowdy men."

"No doubt he prefers the home-cooked meals and the company of its lovely proprietress, as well," Grace mused silkily.

"Is there something you want to ask me right out?" Lilly had never been one for dancing around a subject.

"Indeed I do." Her sister grinned. "Is there anything of the romantic sort brewing between you and our handsome new blacksmith?"

Lilly resumed fiddling with the piano keys to avoid maintaining eye contact with her sister. "He asked me to marry him."

Grace gave a squeal of shock. "Why, Lilly Byrd! You've been holding out on me!" She drew back in mock outrage. "Letting me run on and on about how you need to cut back your work hours in order to socialize more, when all the while you've been juggling two beaux right there at the boarding house."

Lilly sniffed. "I wouldn't call either of them that."

"I would, and I did!" Her sister leaned closer. "Now give me all the details."

Dan waited until he was scheduled to deliver two newly repaired irons to Magnolia before donning the shirt she'd made for him. He'd tried it on a few times, but it was the first day he was actually planning to wear it.

He couldn't help marveling how well it fit. How had the sassy little seamstress known his dimensions? The dark blue fabric was sturdy and warm. It looked nice, too. It wasn't until he was tucking it in that he felt the message she'd embroidered on it. He lifted the hem and read.

Made by a friend for a friend.

He thoughtfully lowered the hem, realizing just how wrong he'd been about Magnolia Byrd. Beneath her frivolous ruffles and lace was a beautiful heart. She was cheeky and outspoken, but kind and generous. She was also so lovely that she took his breath away. It sort of killed him to know that he'd become yet another sorry sap who was secretly besotted with her. *Ah, well.* It couldn't be helped. He figured it was something he'd just have to learn to live with.

Wanting to be certain she saw him wearing his new shirt, he opted to leave his coat on its hook while he dashed through the narrow, snowy alley to her shop. He let himself inside, amused by the tinkling of the bell she'd mounted on the door.

"I'll be right with you," she called in a muffled voice from the back of the room.

Though he'd been inside her shop before, this was the first time he'd really paid attention to his surroundings. There were dress forms in the front window, cascading with wintery fabrics and adornments. A pair of velvet chairs formed a tiny seating area in the front of the shop. In the center of the room was a dressing mirror mounted on a short platform. He could only presume that was where she did her measurements. Against one wall was a pair of sewing machines. Flanking them was a waist-high cabinet upon which her irons were rowed up.

He strode across the room to set the newly repaired ones with the others. Then he turned to the most interesting feature of the room, a Christmas tree. She'd strung red berry garlands around its pine boughs. It added a festive feel to the room.

"It fits!" Magnolia clapped her hands excitedly as she stepped into the room. She walked around him, admiring his new shirt.

"Like a glove," he admitted. "How did you know my dimensions?"

Her smile widened. "A seamstress does not share all of her secrets."

"Was the message on the hem for me, as well?"

"It was."

"So in addition to being allies, we now have to be friends?" he teased.

Though he'd planned to keep his feelings neutral throughout their encounter, the way her blue eyes softened tugged at his heart.

"We don't have to, but I want to." She paused in front of him to tip up her heart-shaped face as she spoke.

Her bluntness surprised him. "I've not been friends with many women before." None, in fact. "So you might need to spell out what this means." He held his breath while he waited for her to answer.

"Let's see." Her eyes sparkled merrily. "A truly good friend would be loyal and dependable. Oh, and he would be obsessed with pleasing me."

Huh? His breath huffed out in a chuckle as he perceived she was roasting him. Again. "Sounds like you're describing a lap dog."

"Not at all." Her voice was innocent. "A simple lap dog would never be able to sharpen my scissors or mend the handles of my irons." She sashayed a step closer as she spoke.

He shrugged to hide his confusion. "Call me loco, but it sounds like you're asking for more than friendship."

"Is that going to be a problem for you, cowboy?"

What? He stared at her in astonishment. So she *did* want more than friendship? *Mercy!* "No, ah…" His heart pounded as he replayed her words in his head, trying to make sense of them. Was it his imagination, or was the stunningly beautiful Magnolia Byrd truly asking him to be her man? "You want a fellow obsessed with pleasing you, eh?"

"Not just any fellow." Her voice was husky. "You."

Well, I'll be! In that moment, she could have reached out with her little pinky finger and knocked him clean over. "All the spoiling and pleasing you want is going to have to happen on a blacksmith's budget," he warned, finally daring to reach for her hand.

Her fingers curled warmly against his as if they'd been made to fit together.

"Fair enough. What do you have in mind?" she taunted. "Since you scoffed at the notion of plucking a pitiful flower or two."

"This." He palmed her cheek. "It's your last chance to run, lass."

"You don't scare me, Dan."

"That is very good to know." His mouth descended on hers.

Chapter 8: Iron Ring

GRAHAM

Neither Graham nor Dan received an invitation to Mr. Lee Davenport's exclusive holiday gathering.

"He's inviting the closest friends of the family, eh?" Dan shook his head as he pumped the bellows, sending red hot flames shooting up from the firebox on the hearth.

"That's what I heard." Normally Graham couldn't have cared less who a pompous gentleman of leisure invited to his next party. However, he wasn't too thrilled about the rumors flying around that Davenport intended to propose to Lilly the same evening. It seemed to Graham that a public display like that could only be intended for one purpose — to put undue pressure on her to accept the cad's suit.

"Then he's not very well versed on who their friends are."

"What? You got excluded, too?" Graham teased. Surely, his apprentice hadn't been expecting to be invited. He and Magnolia had been scrapping like wet cats, both publicly and privately, since the day they'd met. Though Graham had his suspicions about the real reason they argued so much, most folks probably wouldn't view the two of them as anything close to friends.

"I reckon the mistake is understandable." Dan used a set of long-handled tongs to pick up a small stick of iron no bigger than a toothpick. He held it in the flames until it glowed red. "Magnolia and I only started courting a few days ago."

Graham glanced up from the set of wagon wheel spokes he was assembling on their workbench. "Miracle of miracles! You and Magnolia Byrd finally settled your differences." He was happy to hear it, but he wasn't too surprised.

Dan shot him a crooked grin. "A few of them, I reckon. I wouldn't want to settle all of them at once, though. Life would become way too dull."

Graham gave a bark of laughter. "Would you like me to inform Mr. Davenport of his error, or would you like to have the honor of doing so yourself?"

"Great balls of fire! Neither. Let the matter be." Dan transferred the tiny glowing red stick of iron to the forge. Using one of the smallest hammers in their collection, he began to tap it into shape.

Graham watched him with interest, wondering what he was making that required such delicate precision work. "Do you mean to tell me you have no interest in donning your Sunday best suit and enjoying an entire evening of Mr. Davenport's regaling horse tales?"

"That's precisely what I mean. He sounds like a buffoon every time he opens his mouth. I'm not buying his so-called expertise with horses, either."

"Why is that?"

"Where do I begin?" He scowled over the iron ring he was forming. "For one thing, he yanks on his horse's bit like an amateur. He also swings his riding crop like he thinks he's at the races instead of riding down Main Street."

"The races, you say?" Graham's thoughts churned through a conversation he'd overheard the other day between Davenport and a local chap. They'd been sitting at a table in the middle of Lilly's dining room, talking and laughing a little too loud for his tastes. And they'd been debating the merits of horse racing, of all things.

"That's what I said." Dan paused his tapping long enough to exchange the hammer he'd been using for an even smaller one. "He can spout all sorts of facts about the country's top racing horses. He knows their names, their top run times, even their recent injuries. But put him anywhere near a real flesh and blood horse, and he can barely tell the front end from the back end."

"Interesting." Though Dan had a reputation for being a hothead, Graham knew it was mostly because he tended to speak his mind. He didn't sugar-coat the truth, something Graham had always appreciated about him. "So you don't believe he's the horseman he claims to be?"

"I know he's not. My gut says he's more accustomed to sitting in a carriage than a saddle."

Graham's suspicions grew horns. If Davenport was lying about his expertise with horses, what else was he lying about? "I've always thought there was something off about the fellow. Just can't quite put my finger on what it is. I sent a few telegrams to friends back home, hoping someone might know something about him." It troubled him to no end that he'd not heard back yet. He was running out of time.

Dan squinted at the piece of iron he was still tapping and shaping. "What exactly are you hoping to accomplish?"

Graham shrugged. "I'd mostly like to verify he's who

he says he is. I contacted the sheriff's office in Savannah, along with that blacksmith friend of ours who relocated to Charleston."

"Ah. I think I know what this is really about." Dan sounded smug as he held up his creation in the air to examine it.

Graham was surprised to note that his rough and tough apprentice had formed a small, delicate ring. "You do?"

"You're trying to eliminate the competition."

Graham waggled his brows. "That would certainly be a welcome side-benefit if it turns out that Davenport is up to no good."

"Have you heard back from anyone yet?"

"No." Graham adjusted the iron spokes in front of him. "When I do, I might just find out he's everything he says he is — a wealthy young gentleman on the lookout for a beautiful wife." Graham couldn't condemn him for that.

Dan stomped back to the fire and dipped the ring in the flames a second time. "I can tell you one thing you're not going to find out about him."

"Do tell all."

"You're not going to hear of any glorious exploits involving horses. His prowess in the saddle is all stuff and nonsense, mark my words."

Convinced he had each wagon spoke in its optimal spot, Graham lifted the first one with a pair of tongs and carried it to the fire. It was time to weld them together. "I reckon he wouldn't be the first young dandy to exaggerate his skills a bit."

"Maybe not," Dan growled, "but it sure gets my dander up that he's trying to impress a woman with skills he doesn't possess. Just for the record, we aren't the only ones who think he's a fool. Magnolia told me she wouldn't marry him if he was the last man on earth."

"I don't think Lilly's too impressed with him, either," Graham mused as he stared into the flames. "For the life of me, I can't fathom why she even pretends to be."

"Magnolia says it's just how her older sisters are — all three of them. Always making sacrifices for each other. According to her, Elizabeth signed up to become a mail-order bride just so their widowed ma would have one less mouth to feed. Grace did the same thing a year later, hoping to raise enough funds to save them from poverty. Apparently, Elizabeth did a little interfering behind the scenes to ensure that their childhood friend, Lieutenant Charley Arrington, would be the one waiting for her at the altar. And now Lilly has it in her thick head — Magnolia's words, not mine — that she owes it to their ma to at least consider Davenport's offer to return them to the home they lost during the war."

Plus, she'd promised her dear friend, Widow Gable, that she'd stop turning up her nose at every male who looked her way. Graham was none too thrilled about Davenport's tactics in keeping her attention, though. "What he's doing feels rather like bribery to me. Or black-mail. I wouldn't be able to live with myself if I treated any woman like that." He shook his head. "Holding something hostage that's dear to her and demanding that she marry him before giving it back. It's despicable."

"So what are you going to do about it, boss?"

"I'm going to continue wooing her the honest way." That, and pray that he received a telegram back soon. Graham wasn't sure what else he could do. He also planned to continue making himself as useful to her as he could around the boarding house. He hoped to eventually become someone she couldn't bear the thought of living without.

He watched Dan from the corner of his eye as he employed various bores and picks to etch a design along the ring he'd formed. "What are you making over there?"

"A ring," his friend announced in satisfaction.

Graham's brows shot upward. "For what?"

"For the woman I plan to marry."

Graham gave a whoop of delight and set down his tongs. "Why, Dan Forest! You sly dog! If I hadn't asked, how long were you planning on keeping this from me?"

"Just until she says yes."

"Well, when are you going to ask her?"

"As soon as possible."

Christmas Eve

The next opportunity didn't present itself until a few hours before Davenport's holiday party. Dan had been anxiously watching the east window of the blacksmith's shop for the last few days. It was the one that faced the seamstress shop, where Magnolia had kept a steady flood of customers coming and going. At the first break in traffic, when he thought he might have a chance to catch her alone, he flew to her front door only to discover she was doing a dress fitting for a friend.

Magnolia peeked at him from beneath her long, blonde lashes as she pinned the hem of the dress. "Oh, hello there, Mr. Forest."

He raised his hand awkwardly in greeting.

"How can I help you, sir?" she continued cheerfully.

Realizing she was keeping things professional for the

benefit of their listener, he mumbled, "I'll come back later."

She nodded. "In about two hours, I'll be able to give you my undivided attention."

He scowled at her mantle clock as he fingered the iron ring in his pocket. In two hours, she'd be closing down her shop to head to that highfalutin dinner party at her sister's house. As he hesitated, Magnolia turned her client away from the dressing mirror and stepped back. Then she peeked out from behind the woman and blew him a kiss.

He was too astonished to immediately respond. She looked like a princess this afternoon in a gown of mauve and ivory wool.

"Two hours, Mr. Forest," she repeated firmly.

"Yes, ma'am." Drinking her in with his gaze, he slowly backed from the shop.

Fortunately, Graham was out on a call, doing an emergency re-shoeing for a local rancher's horse. It was just as well that he was gone, because Dan was in no mood to explain his state of agitation, nor his many impatient glances at the clock. To his relief, Magnolia's customer left well before the two hours were ended. He wasted no time in jamming on his Stetson and marching next door again.

The door jingled its usual greeting. He irritably reached up and silenced the bell. Then he deliberately turned Magnolia's Open sign to Closed and locked the door behind him. Good gravy, but his woman was turning out to be a hard woman to pin down for a moment alone.

"Who's there?" she called from somewhere in the back regions of her shop.

"Mr. Forest. I'm here for my appointment," he called back.

"You're early." Her chuckle held a thread of stress.

"I was hoping to catch you before you head to your dinner party."

"I'm glad you did. Now you can escort me there yourself." She finally stepped out from behind the curtained-off part of the room. "What do you think of this dress?"

The sight of her knocked the breath clean out of his lungs. "It's really something." The ivory gown she had on made her look like a bride. His bride, Lord willing. She'd embroidered tiny green vines along the hem of her wrists and ankles.

"I thought you didn't care for fancy dresses," she teased.

"Maybe I wasn't talking about the dress." He closed the distance between them and stood before her, utterly enchanted. He could've happily done nothing but gaze at her the rest of the night. She was that stunning.

Her bluebonnet eyes took on a tremulous sheen. "Sometimes you say just the right things, Dan Forest."

"Have to keep my girl on her toes."

"Two can play that game." She reached up to twine her arms around his neck. "I bet you can't tell me what I'm thinking right now."

He slid his arms around her slender frame and tugged her closer. "I reckon you're thinking about all the things that need patched and mended on me."

She smiled despite the dampness in her eyes. "Always, but that's not the only thing I'm thinking right now."

"You're also probably gloating about how well my new shirt fits."

"I most certainly am." She lightly combed her fingers through the hair waving against the back of his neck. "Have I told you yet how handsome you look in blue?"

"I'd rather you not." He felt his ears turn red.

"You don't like compliments." Her voice softened.

"I don't."

"Something tells me you haven't had many of them."

He tipped his forehead against hers. "I was raised in an orphanage. What do you think?"

"I think," she said softly, "that you're going to have to suffer through another compliment or two from me in the coming days."

"You've always been skilled at making me suffer, lass."

"That's what you get for courting a seamstress, Mr. Forest. Before long, you're going to be the best dressed man in town."

"Say it isn't so," he pleaded, lifting his head. He had no interest in being turned into a dandy.

"That's what we're doing, aren't we?" she inquired, sounding suddenly anxious. "Courting?"

He reached behind him to unclasp her hands. Without letting them go, he slowly took a knee before her. "Yes."

"What are you doing, Dan?" she asked nervously.

"What does it look like?" He held her gaze steadily.

"Like you're about to give me a long-overdue apology for all your meanness." Her voice shook a little.

"Is that what you want from me, Magnolia? An apology?"

"Not particularly." Her fingers tightened on his.

"Good, because I figured you've given as good as you've gotten every step of the way." He brushed his thumbs across the tops of her hands. "There's something else I'd much rather ask you."

"What is that?" she whispered.

"Will you marry me?"

"Dan!" Her voice hitched on a breathy sob.

Encouraged by her response, he let go of her hands to reach inside his pocket. Withdrawing the iron vine ring he'd made for her, he slid it on her finger.

"There aren't many folks in the world I trust, Magnolia. Before I met you, it was pretty much just Graham. But despite all the merciless tongue lashings you've dealt me, you managed to lasso my trust and my heart, too. It's yours, now and forever, if you want it."

Tears dripped down her cheeks as she stared in wonder at the ring. "Did you make this for me, Dan?"

"I did. Why? Is it too humble a token for a fancy woman like you?"

She gave him a watery smile. "You know it isn't. It's beautiful work. It's also a perfect match for the dress I have on right now."

He couldn't have been more pleased by her words. "So you intend to wear it?"

"Always." Her gaze shone with unspoken promises. "It looks right on me."

"I agree." He lifted her hand to his mouth and kissed her fingers. "Does this mean I can finally call you Mags?"

She tugged him to his feet. "It means you can kiss me again, cowboy."

Chapter 9: Shocking Discovery

LILLY

When Graham returned from the emergency horse shoeing job, he found a very dazed Dan pacing their shop. He glanced up as Graham shut the door behind him, revealing red-rimmed eyes.

"She said yes," he choked. "Graham, she said yes. To *me*!"

He stared for a second. Then he jogged across the room with his hand outstretched. "Congratulations, my friend!"

Dan slapped his hand aside and embraced him instead. "I wouldn't have made it this far if it wasn't for you, boss. I wouldn't have a job or any training to speak of."

"You've earned everything you are and everything you've become," Graham assured, clapping him on the back. "Though you grumble about a lot of things, work is not one of those things. I couldn't ask for a better partner." He stepped back and sent a playful punch to his shoulder.

Dan pretended to wince. "Apprentice, you mean."

"Future partner, then, after you've completed your training. What do you say to that?"

Dan's chuckle turned hoarse with emotion. "I say my day just keeps getting better."

"Is that a yes?"

"I'm kissing your boots inside my head." He dashed the back of his hand across his eyes. "Since this conversation has already grown sappy, I might as well say you're the closest thing I've ever had to a family. I never met my folks, Graham. I don't even know who they are. But ever since you took me on, I've felt like I had a real—"

"Don't you dare say father!" Graham yelped. "I feel old enough as it is." He shook his head. "Having to watch my still-wet-behind-the-ears apprentice getting married before I do."

"I was going to say you're like a brother."

Graham liked the sound of that immensely. "Now that you mention it, you sure do fit the bill of an ornery younger sibling." He'd always wanted a brother. Alas, the good Lord had only blessed his parents with one son. They'd been seasonal workers, moving from cotton farm to cotton farm wherever they could find work. When they'd succumbed to a fever in his early teens, they'd left him truly alone in the world.

"Eh, well, you don't make a half bad bossy older brother, either."

"Someone has to keep you in line." Graham lunged for his apprentice, hunkering down for the tackle.

Dan was a lot stronger than his wiry frame suggested. They crashed to the floor, wrestling and knocking tools and equipment this way and that.

The front door of the blacksmith shop flew open.

"What in tarnation?" Mags stood there, as dainty as a queen in her ivory gown and fur cape. Her mouth rounded into a perfect O. She stooped to get a closer look at Dan, whom Graham had just finished pinning to the floor.

Sorry, brother. A man my size has certain advantages. He hastily let him go, not wanting to embarrass him further in front of his betrothed.

Smirking, Dan rolled to his feet. "I just finished giving Graham the good news."

"I see." She looked like she was trying not to laugh. "It was my mistake for assuming you were headed to Rose Haven to change into a suit for our dinner party."

He gaped at her. "I didn't realize you were serious about taking me to that thing."

She held up the hand bearing her engagement ring. "This ring says otherwise. From now on, you're the gentleman who gets the honor of escorting me…" she paused dramatically, "everywhere!" The smile she gave him was blinding.

"Mags, darling," Dan groaned, holding up his hands beseechingly.

"Your current misery does not phase me," she assured cheerfully. "Go change." She pointed at the front door.

"Heartless woman." He shook his head at her, though his eyes were twinkling.

"The food will be superb," she coaxed, "and you'll get to hear me sing."

"Oh, for crying out loud!" Graham gave his apprentice a none-too-gentle shove toward the door. "Quit your sniveling and do as your lovely lady bids." He pretended exasperation for her benefit. "Pray forgive my future partner's lapse in manners. I feel the dropping temperatures have frozen his gray matter."

Her eyes widened. "Future partner? Oh, Dan!" She clapped her hands in excitement. "This is such marvelous news."

Swallowing his envy, Graham rejoiced in the happiness they'd found together. "I know it'll take a little work, but I

JO GRAFFORD, WRITING AS & JOVIE GRACE

don't see why we can't renovate the loft apartment above us and make it habitable. It's humble, but it's not a half bad start for young married folk."

Mags gave a tiny shriek of delight and launched herself into Dan's arms.

None of their eyes were dry by now.

Dan waved him over to their happy huddle, where the three of them shared a round of hugs. It was with great reluctance that Dan finally disengaged himself from the group. "I reckon I've stalled as long as I can. Time to go stuff myself into a miserably uncomfortable suit to keep both my future wife and future partner happy."

"That's the spirit!" Mags returned gaily. She spun impulsively in Graham's direction. "You should come with us."

He frowned. "I never received a formal invitation."

"Neither did Dan. However, Mr. Davenport specifically stated the party was for our closest friends, so it is within my full right to extend an invitation to you now."

He wanted to accept her offer. However, tonight Lee Davenport would likely make his grand and very public marriage proposal. Graham wasn't certain he had the heart to witness another man fawning all over Lilly. "I am honored that you asked, but the invitation really should've come from someone else."

She nodded sadly. "Lilly is the kind of woman you have to be patient with."

Melancholy settled in his chest. "I know." He feared she was also the kind of woman who might require him to prove his love to her by letting her go. Lilly Byrd valued her independence above all else. There was a distinct chance she would never give it up, not even for him. "I thank you again for the invitation, though. It was very kind of you."

With a wry smile, Mags left the shop, clinging to Dan's arm. Graham watched them through the window overlooking the front porch as they headed toward Rose Haven. Letting out a weary breath, he straightened up the shop from his earlier scuffle with Dan. It didn't take long. The two of them had always made a habit of cleaning up after themselves while they worked. Every tool got returned to its proper place after each use.

After picking up the few items they'd knocked over, he swept the floor and dumped the dust and wood chips into the fire. It sparked back to life for a minute or two, then died down again. He swiftly banked it and moved to the front door. Shrugging on his coat and clapping his hat on his head, he stepped outside. The frigid winter breeze immediately surrounded him.

After locking the door of the blacksmith shop, he trudged toward the boarding house. Lilly would be away this evening at Davenport's blasted dinner party, but he had no doubt she'd arranged for someone to serve dinner to her guests in her place.

A few shop owners waved as he tromped past on the snow-packed street. He waved back. It was closing time for most businesses in Cowboy Creek. The boarding house would remain open for those who wanted a hot meal, so would the tavern. The livery down the street almost never closed. However, both sides of Main Street were full of folks heading home for the night.

Snow flurries made their chilly landing on his nose and jaw as he walked. From the corner of his eye, he caught the glimmer of candles on the Christmas tree in the town square. The lighting ceremony had taken place a few weeks ago. This evening, a cluster of carolers from the church choir was standing in front of it. He listened to their reverent voices rise and fall over the beautiful lines of Silent Night.

Normally, Graham enjoyed listening to Christmas songs, but this evening it merely served as a reminder of the holiday dinner and musicale that would be taking place at the Arringtons' mansion. The place where the woman he loved would be proposed to by another man... He couldn't bear the thought of her saying yes. It was going to be a very long night, one that would hold no peace for him until Dan returned to fill him in on what had taken place there.

"You, there!"

Graham heard a man shout, but he kept his head down, using his hat brim to shield his face against the worst slap of the wind. He was still a newcomer in town, so it was unlikely anyone was hailing him at this late hour.

"Mr. Christensen, sir!"

His head came up. To his surprise, the telegraph clerk was hurrying his way, waving a slip of paper in the air. "Yes?"

"I have a telegram for you, sir. It's marked important." The lad handed over the slip of paper.

"Thank you." Heart pounding, Graham held it up in the fading light, wondering if it was the long-awaited for response to his inquiry about Mr. Davenport.

"A goodnight to you, sir!" The telegraph clerk took off at a jog while Graham was still reading.

The message was from his blacksmith friend in Charleston.

Davenport Shipping to disinherit gambler son if not wed by Christmas STOP Lost big at horse races STOP Byrd Plantation

**auction in January STOP Daven-
port bid submitted.**

Graham had to read the contents of the telegram several times before the words fully sank in. It sickened him to learn that Lee Davenport had been outright lying to the Byrd family about so many things. He was not yet in possession of the beloved home they'd lost to creditors, and he could easily lose any chance of ever owning it to a higher bid. Nor was he the horse connoisseur he claimed to be. Far from it! He was nothing more than a shifty, lowdown gambler. He was a disappointment to his family, a man who might lose everything in the coming months if his father followed through on his threat to disown him.

I have to warn Lilly. Graham increased his stride. He'd been officially invited to the holiday party by Mags, so he had every right to make a showing. According to his pocket watch, however, he was already running at least an hour late. He'd probably already missed dinner, and heaven only knew what else he'd missed — hopefully not the big tableau Mr. Davenport had planned for Lilly.

Please, God, help me make it in time to save her the humiliation of that cad's unworthy proposal.

Despite the fact that he smelled like smoke and his clothing was stained with soot, he decided not to waste time returning to the boarding house to change. The clock was ticking. Instead, he bypassed Rose Haven and headed for the livery.

One of the stable lads saddled a horse for him. Another lad gave him directions to the Arrington mansion. "It's a bit off the beaten track, sir. You'd best get there before dark, or you might miss the final turn." He went on to describe a hard-packed drive between two centuries-old spruces. "If you make it all the way to Farmer Jim's place, you've gone too far."

Graham tried to absorb all their advice, but he had no idea what Farmer Jim's place even looked like and didn't take the time to ask. He leaped onto his rented horse and thanked the lads for their assistance. *Show me the way, Lord.*

The snow was coming down harder now, making his gut tighten with apprehension. He'd been counting on following the trail of horses' hooves and wagon wheels for that hard-to-spot final turn. In this weather, however, he was just as likely to end up frozen solid in a snowdrift.

Then again, such thoughts didn't exhibit much faith. Tonight wasn't the time for the faint of heart. Lilly needed him.

Graham dug in his heels. "Come on, boy." He whistled in the hopes of coaxing the horse to go faster. "There's a lovely lady in need of a blacksmith up yonder, and it's up to you to get me there."

The horse tossed his head and whinnied.

"You understood that, eh?" Graham patted the steed's neck and hunkered a little lower behind it in the saddle, trying to preserve as much body heat as possible for the cold ride ahead.

The wind continued to whip at his clothing, and the snow continued to fall. By some miracle, however, he managed to locate the narrow driveway leading uphill to the Arrington mansion. Lights flickered in the distance, confirming that he'd found the right path.

At the top of the hill, a massive stone dwelling towered over him, with candles gleaming from countless windows. A stooped over cowboy ambled in their direction, holding up a lantern. It turned out to be Sam Bullock, making Graham wonder who Lilly had left in charge of the boarding house.

"I reckon it's a good night to be a blacksmith in Cowboy Creek," the grizzled older man rumbled. "Seeing as how both of you wrangled an invitation to the most highfalutin party of the season."

Graham leaped down from his horse and handed over the reins. "It's an honor to be here, sir." He still wasn't certain how well his presence would be received by one lovely lady in particular. However, he was about to find out.

"I'll settle your horse in the stable while you tip up a fancy cup with your fancy friends. It's too cold to keep 'em tethered outside."

"Much obliged, sir."

"Bah!" Old Sam waved away his words. "You can pocket them sirs with my blessing. Sam is the only handle I go by."

Graham tipped his hat brim, which had the unfortunate effect of bringing an avalanche of snow down on his face.

Sam snorted with laughter as he led the horse away.

Good gravy. Graham could no longer feel his nose. However, he waited until he made it up the wide porch stairs to the stone veranda before removing his hat altogether. He slapped it against his leg to remove the rest of the snow that had caked on it during his ride. Then he stomped his boots and rubbed his gloved hands up and down his arms to dislodge the rest of the whiteness from his person.

The front door swung upon, and a smiling face appeared. "Graham! You made it!"

It was Mags. "I thought I saw someone ride up, and I couldn't be happier to discover that someone is you." She pushed open the door. "Come in before you turn into a block of ice."

He gratefully followed her inside. "I need to speak to Lilly." His lips were stiff from cold, making his words come out somehow slurred. "Please."

She reached for his coat, but he waved away her assistance. "There's no need. I won't be staying long."

"Suit yourself," she sighed. "No doubt you're wondering, so I'll go ahead and say it. He hasn't proposed yet."

Graham filled his lungs with the toasty warm air filling the foyer and gave it a few seconds to thaw his insides before exhaling. "I really just came to speak to Lilly. If you'd be so kind to let her know I'm waiting in the hall."

Ignoring his pleas, Mags tugged him farther into the house, towards the sounds of merriment.

"No, I...please, Mags. I'm not dressed to go in there." He grew silent as she nudged him inside an enormous drawing room.

A pair of gold and crystal chandeliers flickered above their heads, weighed down with too many candles to count. Before him was a blur of ladies in elegant gowns and men in impeccable suits, all of whom seemed to be staring at him. Velvet sofas were scattered throughout the room, and a Christmas spruce graced the far wall against a backdrop of bookshelves.

Dan was standing by the mantle, looking uncomfortable with the gold handle of a delicate teacup pinched between his thumb and forefinger. He straightened as he caught sight of Graham, looking both startled and concerned. As he pushed away from the mantle, Graham gave him a subtle head shake, stopping his approach.

His gaze hastily sought out Lilly. He found her seated at a pianoforte on the far side of the room with Mr. Lee Davenport hovering at her elbow. The scoundrel took one look at Graham, and his expression grew grim. He bent closer to Lilly and spoke something directly into her ear.

Her startled gaze flew to the doorway.

Graham felt it the moment their gazes clashed. It was like a punch in the gut, painful but far sweeter.

Though she paled a few degrees, her fingers didn't stop moving over the piano keys, filling the room with the notes of a familiar Christmas tune. She was wearing a gown of ice blue fabric that matched her eyes. It was edged in several rows of lace at the neck, and buttons glinted like pearls on her bodice. Her blonde hair was twisted high with a few stray ringlets resting against her cheeks. She looked nothing like a boarding house proprietress tonight and everything like the southern belle she'd been raised to be.

For the span of a few heartbeats, Graham's resolve faltered. The winter cold from his ride to the mansion seemed to be clawing its way inside his very soul. *I do not belong here.* The only family he'd ever known he'd lost years ago. Back when they were alive, though, they'd never celebrated Christmas in this kind of opulence. They would've counted themselves fortunate to have a loaf of bread and a block of cheese to pass around.

Though the drawing room was full of people, he suddenly felt alone.

Without dropping his gaze, Lilly parted her lips and began to sing.

> *"I heard the bells on Christmas day*
> *Their old familiar carols play*
> *And mild and sweet their songs repeat*
> *Of peace on Earth, good will to men."*

Graham's breath left his lungs as he listened to her voice echo sweetly around the room. She had a real gift. The music seemed to flow straight from her heart to her hands and tongue. It was like listening to an angel play and sing.

Her three sisters stepped closer to her, fanning around the pianoforte as they joined their voices with hers on the chorus. She sang the first part of the line, and they harmonized at the end of each line.

> *"And the bells are ringing, peace on Earth*
> *Like a choir they're singing, peace on Earth*
> *In my heart I hear them, peace on Earth*
> *Peace on Earth, good will to men."*

When Lilly launched into the second verse, Graham discovered that he didn't want the song to end. He never wanted to stop being enchanted by the rise and fall of her voice. It gave him hope and made him believe in things like miracles all over again.

He pressed a hand to his heart, feeling like Heaven itself was touching down.

As the last notes of the song died, he was dimly aware of Mrs. Byrd wiping her eyes. She held out her arms to the four lovely singers. "My beautiful daughters!"

Lee Davenport swaggered out from behind the pianoforte. "I think this is the perfect time—"

"To make our announcement," Mags interrupted breathlessly, stepping away from her sisters.

"I, er…what?" He frowned slightly at her.

Mags hurried to Dan's side and reached for his hand. "This wonderful man asked me to marry him, and I said yes." She tugged him toward the center of the room, fluttering her engagement ring in the air for all to see.

"You're marrying a blacksmith?" Mr. Davenport's horrified expression suggested that he didn't think she could do any worse.

Her sisters gathered around her as if they hadn't heard his outburst. They made girlish squeals of amazement as they reached for Mags' hand. To his credit, Dan never left her side, though he looked vastly uncomfortable to be the object of so much attention.

Miranda Byrd glided over to him, an older version of her daughters with strands of silver woven through her once-blonde hair. "I could not be happier by the news." She stood on her tiptoes to embrace him. "Welcome to the family, Dan."

With a furious glare in Graham's direction, Lee Davenport stalked up to Lilly. Reaching for her hand, he tugged her a little away from her sisters and dropped ceremoniously to one knee.

"My beloved Lilly," he intoned.

She cast an agonized look over her shoulder at Graham.

Something inside him snapped. "Enough," he said harshly. Stalking in their direction, he gestured for the kneeling scoundrel to rise. "Get up," he commanded. "You've no right to so much as polish the dust off her shoes."

The young dandy stared at him in shock for a moment before howling, "How dare you speak to your betters in such a manner, you filthy wretch." He was so overcome with fury that he stumbled as he rose to his feet. "I'm of a mind to teach you a lesson you'll never forget."

"How about we take this outside?" Graham offered coldly. "That'll give you a chance to explain why you are not, in fact, the owner of the Byrds' family home in Charleston, as you claim to be."

"Not yet," Davenport snapped, "but I will be soon. I'm in the process of purchasing it."

"It may happen, and it may not," Graham corrected.

"I've been informed that the bank is putting it up for auction in January. Who knows? Maybe I'll enter a bid for the place myself."

"As if you could afford such a thing," the man sneered.

"You're right. I can't, but neither can you. According to my sources, you gambled away your fortune at the races. You're about to be disinherited altogether if you don't marry and settle down from your wild ways by Christmas. That's the real reason you traveled to Cowboy Creek, is it not? Out of cowardice and self-preservation, not out of any real altruism toward a family who's already suffered enough."

A shocked silence met Graham's words. To his alarm, Davenport reached inside his dinner jacket. Graham caught a glimpse of silver as he drew out a handgun.

Dan's arm moved so quickly that Graham saw little more than a blur as he twisted the gun away and held the barrel towards the ceiling.

A collective sigh of relief rose from those gathered.

"It's not even loaded," Davenport whined, as he perceived the varying degrees of horror and censure on the faces of those surrounding him. "I only meant to scare him a bit."

The gentlemen in the room converged on him, and he was led, protesting loudly, from the room. The ladies drifted after them, leaving Graham facing Lilly alone.

"My deepest apologies for that display." He inclined his head humbly. "Pray believe me when I say I did not come here to destroy your Christmas."

She shook her head, making the elegant curls dance against her cheeks. For some reason, the gesture made his heart ache all the more.

"No," she said softly. "It appears that you came to save it."

"Lilly," he cried hoarsely, overcome by the realization that she wasn't angry with him, after all.

They reached for each other at the same time. She wrapped her arms around him and rested her head against his chest. "You were right about him. I've been such a fool."

"He was right about one thing, at least. I *am* filthy," Graham confessed roughly against her hairline. "Have a care, lass. I don't want to mess up your dress."

She tipped her face up to his. "I don't give a fig about this dress. What I do care about is that you risked freezing to death to save me from a lifetime of humiliation and misery."

His heart sank. "Did you truly mean to accept his proposal, then?"

"Of course not!" she snapped. "I was only speaking hypothetically, but that doesn't diminish the magnitude of what you did for me tonight."

"Even though I don't belong here, I decided that I love you too much to stay away." He gazed down at her help-lessly. "I've loved you since my first encounter with your sass. I know that's hardly a romantic thing to say. I wish I was capable of spouting the kind of poetry you deserve, but I'm just a lowly blacksmith. That's all I'll ever be. I'm not worthy of you. Of this." He glanced around them at the glittering room.

"Are you finished?" she inquired crisply.

"Almost. I also wanted to tell you how sorry I am for my selfishness. You've repeatedly informed me how much you value your career and the financial freedom it has given you. And like a bumbling blacksmith, I've run roughshod over your words again and again. But no longer. I'm listening tonight. Very closely. If you tell me again that you value your independence over being tied down to any man, I will withdraw my request. My heart will always belong to you, but your happiness means more to me than—"

"Please stop," she commanded softly.

He halted his remorseful tirade in confusion.

"I do value my independence, Graham, but I also value things like honesty, bravery, and loyalty — all of which you demonstrated this evening. My head is telling me to stick to my original plan of remaining a spinster. However, my heart keeps telling me that having and holding a love like yours might just be worth giving up a little of my freedom." Her voice trembled with earnestness.

His heart leaped with so much joy that it nearly blinded him. "What are you saying, Lilly?"

"I'm saying yes. Yes, I will marry you."

He cupped her face in his large hands. "Am I dreaming, or is this really happening?"

Her blue eyes sparkled with wickedness. "Perhaps you should kiss me to be sure."

He needed no more urging. His head descended, and Heaven finished touching down when his lips brushed hers.

Epilogue

One year later

Lilly stared out the window overlooking her kitchen sink at Rose Haven, filled with wonder at how quickly her first year of marriage to Graham had flown past. It was another snow-drenched Christmas Eve. The ground stretched whitely behind the glass panes, tinged the faintest shade of rose by the setting sun.

This year she'd closed Rose Haven early for a private celebration in the dining room. Her family and their dearest friends would be in attendance, along with her boarders. She'd been cooking for two straight days in preparation.

The boarding house was full, as usual, and had stayed full the entire year. The few times a room had opened up, it was filled before nightfall. *Good gracious!* She actually had a waiting list these days. Graham was talking about building an addition that would double the number of rooms they had to rent, as well as expand their own living quarters. He'd sold his cabin and property across town the moment it was built and used the funds to purchase the empty lot behind Rose Haven.

His blacksmith business was booming, thanks to his hard work and Dan's tremendous assistance. They already acted like partners, even though Dan had two years left of his apprenticeship before the guild would issue his credentials.

Mother was happy that all four of her daughters were married to fine, upstanding men they loved, who loved them in return. She'd altogether stopped talking about returning to Charleston someday. Her life and everything that mattered most to her was in Cowboy Creek now. It didn't hurt her level of contentment one bit that Mags and Dan had given her twin granddaughters a few months earlier or that Grace and Charley had just announced they were expecting their first child.

A soft sigh escaped Lilly. The Lord had blessed her in so many ways. Nevertheless, Christmas this year was over-shadowed by a sadness she couldn't seem to shake. Her hand crept to her still-flat belly. It was starting to feel as if one dream of hers, in particular, was never going to come true.

She longed to help Graham create the family he'd always dreamed of having. So far, though, she'd not been able to conceive. As each month passed, the possibility that she might not ever be able to have children filled her with increasing despair.

Though Graham never complained about her barren state, she knew he had to be disappointed.

"Please, God," she whispered into the empty room. "We want a family of our own so badly."

A commotion outside the window interrupted her prayer. To her surprise, Graham was dragging something through the snow, something that appeared to be alive. The scrawny creature was wrestling like a feisty kitten, but to no avail. He was no match for Graham's bearish size and strength.

Lilly ran to the side door and yanked it open. "What in tarnation is going on out here?"

Though Graham was blustering at the creature, as they grew closer she could tell he was only pretending to bluster. His hat was missing, his auburn hair wind-tossed. Raw concern infused his green gaze as he beheld the lad in his arms.

"You are not going to believe this," he exploded in feigned outrage as he crossed the threshold with his burden. "I just caught us a horse thief."

"A horse thief!" Lilly held a hand over her lips to muffle a chuckle. The lad he'd collared couldn't be more than seven or eight-years-old. His freckled face was pale beneath the patches of dirt mottling it, and his tangled hair was a startling shade of red that nearly matched her husband's.

"Indeed." Graham pulled out a stool in front of the hearth and nudged the shivering lad onto it. His overalls were threadbare, and his boots nearly worn through the toes. He had no coat, though he was wearing a rather impressive number of shirts. "I feared I'd have to call the sheriff and his entire posse of deputies to hunt down this villain. Alas, the stolen horse stumbled on a tree root and foiled his own heist."

Lilly frowned as she struggled to follow Graham's strange tale. Unless she was mistaken, he was attempting to make the little urchin sound like a criminal of legendary proportions.

"What do you have to say for yourself, sirrah?" Graham demanded.

The lad crossed his scrawny arms in belligerence. "I almost got away with it, mister."

"What? I can't hear you!" Graham bellowed. He motioned discreetly to Lilly as he spoke. "Maybe if we get a mug of milk poured up to wet his throat, we'll be able to make more sense of his ramblings."

Ah. She perceived that her husband wished for her to hydrate the child. He looked as if his last meal hadn't been recent, so she added a few slices of bread and cheese to the tray before setting it on a trestle table near the fire.

Once he had a few bites of food in him, the lad seemed more willing to talk.

"What is your name, son?" Lilly asked gently.

He blinked owlishly at her words. "I dunno for sure. The last farmer who took me in called me George. Most everyone else just hollers *boy* when they need something."

His words tugged every motherly instinct in her. He was awfully young to be so utterly abandoned. A few questions later, he confessed he'd been on his own for quite some time — as far back as he could remember, in fact.

"What would you like to be called?" Lilly pressed.

"I once knew a nice man named Tucker, ma'am. Wouldn't mind being called after him."

"How about Tuck?" she suggested quickly.

He made a scoffing sound. "I really don't see no point in naming me unless you plan to keep me."

She lifted her suddenly damp gaze to Graham's as the lad's words struck just the right chord inside her. "May we, Graham?" *Oh, please! May we?* She couldn't recall wanting anything more than to mother the pitiful creature sitting before them like a prisoner on trial.

"Well, now." Graham scratched his chin and pretended to consider the matter. "Might want to clean him up a bit first to see exactly what we're getting ourselves into." He proceeded to help her draw a bath for the lad in a galvanized steel tub. As they set it before the fire, Graham deliberately covered her hands with his.

Thank you, he mouthed.

Though Tuck looked dubiously at the water, he didn't put up much of a fuss when Graham jammed his thumb at it. The water was brown with dirt and soap scum when he finished bathing and toweled off.

Graham left the room and returned with a long-sleeved shirt and an oversized pair of overalls that made the boy smirk. "I reckon I'll grow into it," he assured in the deepest voice he could muster.

In a few years, maybe. Swallowing a sigh, Lilly made a mental note to have Mags tailor some properly fitting clothes for him at the soonest opportunity.

"Really and truly, Graham, what would it take to keep him here at Rose Haven?" she hissed, pulling him aside while Tuck dried his hair by the fire.

"I'll have to ask around, precious. I imagine there'll be paperwork involved to make it official." He frowned in concern at her. "I don't want to get the cart before the horse, though. The little scoundrel nearly rode off with one of our mares."

"I know, but he's a boy without a home, and we're…" She broke off the rest of what she was about to say and reached for his hands. "Right before you showed up with our darling little horse thief, I was begging the Lord to send us a child. This isn't quite what I had in mind, but…"

"Come here, lass." Graham folded her in his arms. "As our pastor likes to say in all his sermons, the Lord moves in mysterious ways His wonders to perform. Maybe there's more to this than a horse-napping, after all."

Her lower lip trembled as she rested her head against

his broad shoulder. "I know how badly you've always wanted a family, Graham."

His arms tightened around her. "And I have one. A fine one."

Though his words soothed the rawest parts of her heart, Lilly wasn't finished. "We've always been honest with each other. You don't have to hide your disappointment from me."

"Disappointment!" He tipped her chin up to gaze down at her in astonishment. "What in the world do I have to be disappointed about?"

The fact that he had to ask made her smile. "About not having a baby of our own," she murmured ruefully.

"Huh." His astonishment didn't immediately clear from his features. "I have experienced many emotions in the first year we've been blessed to spend together. Disappointment isn't one of them, lass."

The heaviness in her heart lifted a few more degrees. "It's just that we never talk much about having a baby, even though I know we're both thinking about it constantly."

"I don't talk about it, because the topic always seems to make you sad," he informed her gently.

"It does," she admitted. "I love you so much, Graham. I don't want you to ever regret marrying me."

"That's not possible." His tone was so vehement that she blinked. "It's not," he added more quietly. "I thank God every morning I wake up next to you and every moment we get to spend together. I also pray every day that you never come to regret giving up your independence to wed me."

"I do not regret it," she breathed, "and I never will. How could you say such a thing?"

His sudden sharp expulsion surprised her. She followed his gaze and gasped along with him.

Tuck was about to nod off to sleep atop his stool, which would surely send him tumbling to the floor.

"Let's find some place for him to rest," she urged as they hurried across the room together.

"Good idea." Graham swept the lad up in his arms, damp hair and all.

As his tangled red locks landed against Graham's broad shoulder, he mumbled, "I don't want to be a horse thief no more. I think I'd rather be on the right side of the law."

"A wise decision, son." Graham grinned as he carried him to the sofa in the back parlor that adjoined their suite.

"There you have it." Lilly gave a soft chuckle. "His run of villainy seems to have vanished with his hunger."

"So it seems." Graham reached over to ruffle the lad's hair. "I run a blacksmith shop, Tuck. We could probably use a junior partner, if you stick around long enough to train with us."

"I like trains," the boy answered sleepily. His eyes remained closed.

Lilly grabbed a quilt off the rack against the wall and hurried back to the sofa to drape it over him. "Rest up, little blacksmith," she whispered. He was going to need his strength for the Christmas party she had planned for later that evening.

His breathing had already evened in sleep.

"Oh, Graham!" Lilly threw her arms around her husband. "He's the best Christmas present ever!"

Mags fretted in front of the dressing mirror she'd installed in their loft apartment. "My figure is ruined," she mourned to her husband. "Utterly ruined."

Dan glanced up from the bench at the foot of their bed, where he was polishing his boots. "I disagree. The last time I checked, you were still the most beautiful woman in Cowboy Creek." The look he gave her was beyond besotted. "And the best dressed."

"You're just saying that to be nice." She continued to pout at her reflection.

He snorted. "Me? Nice?"

She chuckled. "You may have a point." Then she grew pensive again. "But really, Dan. There's this horrible bump I'm afraid I'll never get rid of." She ran a hand in dismay over the curve of her belly.

"Come here." He scowled at her. "Let me take a look at it."

With a sigh, she moved across the room to stand in front of him. "See?" She arched her back to emphasize the area that was causing her so much distress.

"Ah. I think I see the problem." He reached for her hand, using it to tug her closer.

"You do?" she sounded hopeful.

"Sure do." He dipped his head to place a row of kisses across her belly. "There. Problem solved. I haven't gotten to do that all day. Or this." He stood and pulled her into his arms. "Mags, honey. You're so beautiful, before and after having my babies," he assured in a fierce voice as he nuzzled his way across her cheek to her lips, "that you take my breath away."

The whimper of an infant wafted up to them from the blacksmith shop below.

Mags clutched his shoulders. "Our babies," she sighed

against his mouth. "I should go." However, she didn't immediately leave his arms.

"Your mother is on duty." Miranda Byrd had arrived a couple of hours ago to help tend the twins. She insisted it was so Mags would have the proper time to bathe and dress for the Christmas Eve dinner Lilly was serving at Rose Haven. However, Dan knew better. She was anxious to hold her newest grandbabies. "Trust me. She has things well in hand downstairs."

"They might be hungry, though."

"So am I." He dipped his head to capture her lips in the tenderest of kisses. "For this." He kissed her again. "And this. And this."

Another baby whimper met their ears.

"How can you resist that sound?" Mags implored. "It's so precious."

"I can't." He let her go so he could pull on his boots and follow her down the stairs. As he watched his wife and mother-in-law coo over his two infant daughters, he reveled in the joy of having a family to call his own at last. There were some days he still had to pinch himself to believe his good fortune.

One hour later

The Byrd sisters enjoyed one of their rare group hugs at the entrance of Rose Haven's dining room. All four of them were wearing gowns designed by their very own Mags. Lilly was keeping an anxious eye on her new table waiter to ensure he kept the beverages filled and the snack foods coming.

Elizabeth waggled a finger in warning at her young

daughter on the other side of the room. The gesture made the toddler step obediently back from the fireplace she'd been playing too close to. After a short lull, the sisters went back to exclaiming over Grace's high-wasted gown that Mags had sewn specifically to hide her blooming middle. Everyone in the room was excited about the newest addition to their growing family.

"Charley wants a son, but I would be just as happy with a mischievous little girl like my niece over there."

The women turned to smile sweetly at the darling child whose attention had been diverted by a kitten dashing around the room. The chase made her white-blonde pigtails wiggle.

Lilly waited until her sisters had finished ooh-ing and ah-ing over Grace, before sharing the news she'd been bursting to tell them since the moment they'd arrived. "I have something to tell you." She drew a tremulous breath.

"Oh?" Her oldest sister, Elizabeth, glanced pointedly at her belly.

Lilly waved a hand at the entrance to the dining room that Graham's broad shoulders were currently filling. Her breath froze in her throat for a second at how handsome he looked in the chocolate brown leather vest Mags had sewn for him. He was wearing it over a snowy white shirt that he'd tucked into his favorite pair of denim trousers.

Of most interest to the onlookers, however, was the hand of the small redheaded boy that was resting in his much larger paw.

"Er, Lilly?" Mags turned to her in puzzlement. "Who is he?"

It was with an overflowing heart that she started to speak. "Everyone, I'd like for you to meet Tuck, the newest member of our household."

She was certain that the once homeless lad was the

answer to a year of tearful prayers, her very own gift from Above. Mama had always called Christmas the season of miracles, but Lilly had never believed it more than she did right now.

Like this book? Leave a review now!

Join Jo's List and never miss a new release or a great sale on her books.

Ready to read another Christmas bride story? Check out **BRIDE FOR THE INNKEEPER,** *book #1 in the* **Mail Order Brides of Christmas Mountain** *trilogy. He's a by-the-book kind of fellow. She's a rule-breaker. Since opposites attract, sparks fly the moment they meet!*

Sneak Preview: Bride for the Innkeeper

January, 1892 — La Casa foothills, Texas

"I heard they struck gold on Christmas Mountain." The General Store owner's voice turned hoarse with excitement. "Not that I believe every rumor that flies though my shop, but I'm inclined to believe this one." Mav's gravelly voice dropped to a conspiratorial tone that only the two of them could hear.

He'd introduced himself as Maverick Peterson, but everyone who'd shouted a greeting to him in the last few minutes had called him Mav. "What with the way they're demandin' an arm and a leg for every square inch of land up that way now." He shook his head in wonder. "Prices shot plumb through the roof a month ago. You're one lucky devil to inherit a prime piece of real estate right smack in the center of it all." He drawled out his words, slurring the last two together to make them sound like *i' tall.*

He angled his shaggy beard in the direction of the front picture window, which just so happened to be facing the mountain.

"I'm looking forward to laying eyes on it for the first time." Edward Remington turned to follow the direction of the man's gaze.

"Shore hope you ain't too disappointed in the inn itself, son." The older man gave him a measured look.

"Meaning what, sir?" Edward met his gaze squarely, but the store owner was momentarily distracted by a question from another customer. The Mexican man was wearing a wide sombrero and didn't appear to know English. He was using gestures to communicate the fact that he needed to purchase milk for a baby.

While Edward waited for Mav to finish assisting the fellow, he returned his attention to the mountain. As he was on his initial stagecoach journey into town, he was impressed all over again with the majestic beauty of the white-capped peaks on the other side of the glass.

The folks homesteading the surrounding foothills called it Christmas Mountain, but it was actually a whole string of mountains, mostly smaller ones with Christmas Mountain towering above the others in the middle of the range. A low cloud cover was all but hiding its highest peak, making him wonder if it was snowing there right now. His heart raced with excitement at the knowledge that he now owned a piece of the mountain.

Thank you again and again for your generosity, Grandfather. Edward's only regret was that he hadn't boarded a train and traveled this way a year earlier. An attorney by trade, he'd been too busy trying to negotiate his way out of an arranged marriage. Ultimately, all he'd done was gotten himself disinherited by his family. He should have known there'd be no reasoning with his hard-nosed father on the topic of marriage alliances. The man had taken it a step further, called in a favor, and gotten his younger son fired from a thriving law practice, as well.

So if there was any truth to the rumor that someone had struck gold on the mountain where Edward was moving, it could only mean one thing. His luck was about to change.

Folks assumed a lot of things about him, just because he was a Remington, but they were dead wrong. His pockets weren't lined with silver, and everything he and his family touched didn't turn to gold. Well, technically, he *had* been born with a silver spoon in his mouth, thanks to a trust fund his father had turned over to him on his twenty-first birthday, but he'd chosen to walk away and leave it sitting in the bank. Untouched. If his father wanted to launch a legal battle in court to reclaim it, he was more than welcome to. Edward wanted nothing more to do with the man and his manipulative, controlling ways.

From now on, Edward would be charting his own path by the sweat of his brow like every other fellow had to. All he'd brought with him was the small savings he'd earned from his short-lived law practice. And he'd be doing it alone, without the encumbrance of the social climbing bride-to-be his father had picked out for him. She could've cared less who she was marrying, so long as the poor bloke expanded her family's wealth and social consequence. As far as Edward was concerned, she could expand her wealth and position with a husband as shallow as she was. However, that man would not be him.

"About that inn of yours…" Mav Peterson returned to ringing up his purchases with a ferocious scowl, thereby reclaiming Edward's attention. However, he lapsed into silence without finishing the sentence.

"Believe me, my family wasn't too thrilled about me heading west," Edward muttered, hoping to get him talking again. Mav impressed him as a fellow who liked to gossip. Looked like he was going to have to scratch that itch to get any more information out of him.

"Do tell, Yankee!" Mav's bushy brows, which had been furrowed in concern, smoothed a bit, and his silvery eyes twinkled with interest.

"Yes, indeed." Edward lifted his new Stetson to run a hand through his black wavy hair. "They'd be tickled to death if I failed in my attempt to reopen the inn and came running back to New York with my tail tucked between my legs. So if there's anything you can tell me about the inn that'll keep me from giving them that satisfaction, I'd be most obliged."

Mav gave a bark of laughter, practically salivating over that juicy tidbit. "Well, when you put it that a-way…" He finally finished ringing up Edward's lengthy bill on his cash register and listed a total that was twice what he was expecting. Unsure of what all he'd be needing once he arrived at the inn, he was loading his newly purchased wagon with everything he could think of — lanterns and kerosene, dry goods for his pantry, pots and pans, a tool-box, hammers, nails, glue, and at least a dozen other items. It was a lot of shopping, but it still shouldn't have cost near what Mav was claiming.

"Before you start fussing," the shopkeeper grumbled, "I'll have you to know I took it upon myself to throw in a hunting rifle, pistol, holster, and plenty of ammo for both. At your expense, of course." He grimaced. "Ain't no way I'm sending you outta here to face them claim jumpers unarmed."

"Claim jumpers!" Edward spoke louder than he intended, making several heads throughout the store turn in their direction. Lowering his voice, he leaned on the counter, demanding tersely. "What are you talking about, sir?"

Mav shrugged. "Don't blame me for your troubles. I'm just the messenger."

"Fair enough. Still wouldn't mind hearing what you know about these claim jumpers." His move to Christmas Mountain was taking a decidedly complicated turn. Good gravy! He couldn't seem to catch a break.

The store owner nodded and ducked his head closer. "Well, you didn't hear it from me, because I'll deny it if you say you did, but the Hawling brothers have been squattin' on your land the past several months. Probably figured it was abandoned, and who can blame them?" He waved one callused hand. "It's been empty for the better part of a year. Ever since your grandfather passed."

Hawling brothers, eh? Edward made a mental note of the name and braced for their forthcoming confrontation. "Is that the reason for selling me an arsenal? You expect me to ride up there guns a-blazing?" He might not know the first thing about being a pioneer, but that sounded like an awfully foolish plan to him.

"Absolutely not!" Mav Peterson looked horrified. "You'd have a dozen holes in your starched, citified shirt before you could finish drawing that fancy new piece from the holster I just sold ya."

"Good to know," Edward returned dryly. "What exactly are you suggesting, then?"

Mav's expression turned cagey. "Make a stop at the sheriff's office first and get a uniform to ride up there with you. That's your best shot at clearing up the matter of ownership without incurring any casualties."

"I can do that, sir." Either way, Edward wasn't too worried about it. The good Lord had seen fit to direct his grandfather to bequeath him a roof over his head, so it only made sense that the same good Lord would keep him alive while he laid claim to it.

"Alls I'm saying is there's safety in numbers. You'll see what I mean soon enough."

"Appreciate the advice." Edward clapped his Stetson back on.

"Which you didn't hear from me," Mav reminded.

"Indeed, I did not." Edward gave him a wry grin. "Much obliged for my pile of supplies and for everything I didn't hear while you rang them up."

"Now that we can shake on." Mav thrust out a callused paw. "I'm mighty glad your grandpop saw fit to pass down that old place to his kin. We could use some fresh blood around here." He nodded to emphasize his point. "Welcome to Texas, son."

Edward shook his hand heartily.

"Oh, and if you ever need a wife, don't come to me for that, neither." Mav slapped his side and broke into a laugh that made his round belly shake. "Ain't too many marriageable women in these parts, but there's a new mail-order bride agency down the street. According to their advert in the paper, they can hitch you up to a suitable little filly in nothing flat."

Great balls of fire! Ordering a bride through the mail sounded every bit as miserable to Edward as being saddled with the woman his father had arranged for him to marry back east. Though he nodded, he was inwardly breaking into a run. *Thank you, mister, but I think I'll pass on that last suggestion. Women are nothing but trouble.*

He tipped his hat, unsure if Mav was jesting or serious, and gathered up as many supplies as he could carry on his first trip to the wagon. He'd left it parked right outside the store for both convenience sake and security. He figured any would-be horse thieves wouldn't be plying their trade in broad daylight in the middle of Main Street. Or so he hoped.

A silent nod from Mav had the shop boy in the back scurrying their way to help carry another armload. Together, he and Edward got the wagon packed in record time.

Following Mav's advice, he next set his course for the jailhouse he'd driven past on his way from the livery to the General Store. A deputy was seated on the weathered front porch with the legs of his chair tipped back and his boots crossed on the nearby railing. His hat was sliding forward on his nose, and a piece of straw jutted from his mouth.

From the snore rising from beneath his hat brim, Edward perceived he was either on break or sleeping on the job.

"Afternoon there, deputy," he called.

The chair legs came down with a loud thwack, and the hat brim was pushed back. "This better be important," the man growled, "seeing as I was getting in a much-needed siesta after pulling an all-nighter."

A deputy sleeping on the job and anxious to continue doing so. *Interesting.* Edward found himself staring into the curious features of a dusty cowboy, who was no more than a year or two younger than his own five and twenty years. "To me it's important, deputy." He tipped his hat by way of a greeting. "I'm Edward Remington, here to lay claim to my grandfather's inn on the mountain, and—"

The cowboy's guffaw gave him pause. "Shoot! I already knew you weren't from here. I could smell your new hat and boots a mile away." He bounded to his feet and thrust out a gloved hand. "Jesse Hawling."

"Hawling, you say?" Edward's gaze locked on the deputy's laughing one. Unless he was sorely mistaken, that was the same name Mav Peterson had quoted while he was identifying the squatters.

"Yep. I'm the youngest of the three scoundrels in question. Tried to convince my two older brothers not to make too many changes to the place until they could acquire a clean deed, but…" He shook his head, smirking. "Then again, they don't listen much to me or anyone else." He pushed back his hat another inch or so. "If you'd like, I'll ride out there with you and try to talk 'em into moseying now that you've arrived."

Edward frowned in consideration, remembering Mav's warning about the trigger-happy Hawlings. "Not sure I want to put you in that position, considering they're your own kin. Are there any other deputies who might be able to help?"

"Nope. The sheriff's handling a dispute about property lines, and the marshal is dealing with a cattle rustling incident on the north side of town. Though they're in desperate need of more hands on deck, I've yet to convince them to deputize me."

Edward's jaw tightened as he studied the cowboy's fringed suede coat and the frayed hem of his denim trousers. He'd entirely missed the fact that the man wasn't wearing a badge, though the double pistols he was packing gave him the look of a fellow who meant business. "I reckon I jumped to the wrong conclusion with the way you were holding down the porch here." He squinted up at the mountain, wondering if he should head on up there alone.

Several rocky mesas stood between La Casa and Christmas Mountain. A brisk wind whistled across their flat tops, kicking up dust and snow. Edward was glad he'd worn his thickest wool overcoat into town.

Jesse Hawling made a sound of derision and slapped at the air. "I dare say the sheriff appreciates my help, though he's a man of few words. At any rate, I'm all you've got, Remington. No sane person would ride out there to face my brothers alone. Not in this weather, anyway." Without waiting for a reply, he jogged down the short set of porch stairs and leaped atop the wagon seat beside Edward. "Drive."

With his gut shouting that giving Jesse Hawling a ride was a very bad idea, Edward lifted the reins. "Alright, then." He had no idea what he was riding into, and no confidence that having the youngest Hawling at his side would improve his chances of laying claim to his property.

As he drove down the dusty street, a mangy dog shot across his path, making his pair of brown mustangs whinny in protest. He made it to the far side of town without any further incident, however,

Jesse didn't seem to feel the need to fill the air with aimless chatter, though Edward caught him looking over his shoulder to eye the supplies in the back of the wagon.

"Everything alright over there?" Edward asked coolly, hoping he wasn't about to be mugged and robbed.

Jesse snorted. "I'm just trying to figure out why your gun and holster are tossed in the back of your wagon while you're up here driving."

Edward mulled on that for a moment. It certainly didn't sound like his uninvited companion was preparing to rob it. Then again, they'd just met. "Why do you ask?"

"Oh, for crying out loud! Stop the fool horses and arm up, city boy." Jesse threw up his hands. "I said I'd help you deal with my brothers. Didn't mean I was offering to carry your dead carcass on my shoulders."

Edward studied him out of the corner of his eye, amused by the fact that Jesse Hawling was the second man in the space of ten minutes who'd jumped to the incorrect assumption that he was unarmed — all because he hadn't swaggered into town with a holster slung around his midsection the way the locals did.

He reached inside his vest and withdrew the pistol he always traveled with. "Whatever gave you the impression I'm unarmed, Mr. Hawling?"

"Like I said," the man spluttered, twisting around in irritation to view Edward's purchases in the back once again. "You've got a pair of guns lying in plain sight directly behind us, er…" He broke off whatever he was about to say next at the realization he was staring down the barrel of a Derringer.

"Looks can be deceiving, Mr. Hawling."

"Well, I'll be!" Looking more amused than abashed, the cowboy reached up to scratch his chin. "How about you just put that thing away, and we start over? Hello, I'm Jesse Hawling, but you can call me Jesse."

Edward's lips twitched at the new respect glinting in the man's eyes. "I'll call you Jesse if you call me Edward instead of city boy." He pretended to tuck his pistol back inside his vest. Instead he allowed it to slide down the front of his shirt to his waistline, where he retrieved it and pocketed it the moment Jesse glanced away. He preferred to maintain the element of surprise, should he be required to draw his weapon for real next time.

"Just so you know, me and my brothers haven't hurt anyone or anything by pitching our bedrolls in that rundown inn of yours." Jesse's voice and expression were bland as they exited the foothills and started their ascent up the craggy mountain road. "We thought it was abandoned. If anything, our presence kept the real bad guys out."

Real bad guys? Edward gave him a hard look, curious as to who that might be. As far as he was concerned, the Hawling brothers were guilty of breaking and entering, not to mention trespassing. "It was vacant but not abandoned. There's a difference."

"Not much difference that I can see."

"As the rightful owner, I own the deed, pay the taxes, and happen to be driving in that direction to take possession of the property. That's the difference."

Jesse made a face. "If you're looking to sell, I might know of a trio of brothers who'd be more than happy to take it off your hands." He broke into a cackle, as if he'd stated something highly amusing.

"It's not for sale." Edward gave his passenger another sideways glance. Nothing about the cowboy suggested he was a man of means, certainly not one with the capacity to purchase a piece of real estate.

"What do you want with that old place, anyhow?"

Edward raised a brow. "I plan to move in, fix it up, and reopen for business." It was probably going to take his last penny to renovate the inn, so it needed to start earning him a living soon.

Jesse gave a long, low whistle. "Not certain where my brothers and I will go next."

Edward's insides twisted at the thought he'd be pitching the Hawlings out on their ears in the dead of winter. There was only one other possibility he could think of. "You don't, by any chance, know how to swing a hammer, do you?"

"Aw, you old softie!" his passenger mocked. "Are you offering me a job?"

"I'm considering the idea." He slowed his horses as they passed through a busier section of the mountain settlement. "Seems to me it might be simpler than me squaring off against the three of you with pistols."

"Whoa, now!" Jesse's hands came up in protest. "I already told you I'm trying to get deputized. You don't have anything to worry about from me." But he didn't seem in any rush to include his two older brothers in that statement.

"How good are your negotiating skills?" Edward countered.

Jesse grimaced. "So that was your plan all along? Get me to do the yammering and take the first bullet, so you could haul *my* dead carcass down the mountain?"

"Oh, come on! How bad can it be to speak with your own brothers?" Edward stared, genuinely curious at this point.

Jesse gave him a wry smirk. "Guess we're about to find out, eh? I've had a good life. Mostly on the right side of the law."

Mostly, eh? Edward muffled a chuckle. It was an interesting statement coming from a man who harbored hopes of being deputized.

"Only thing I haven't had the pleasure of doing yet is getting hitched. Then again, maybe I shouldn't be in such a hurry. I hear women are nothing but trouble."

You can say that again. "That they are, but you'll be living to explore that dismal fact for yourself. No one is going to die today. You'll get your chance at courting." Edward eyed the upper end of the village they were driving into.

It was built straight into the mountainside. There was a mix of adobe shacks and log cabins lining the inside of the main road, curving its way around the bend, even a few dwellings carved into the rocky cliff walls, themselves. Though there was a light dusting of snow, he could make out the remains of terrace crops that had been hoed and raked into the sandy ground in measured, rectangular intervals. They cascaded down the mountainside as far as the eye could see. There were also clusters of cattle, sheep, and goats grazing in small, fenced-off plats.

"I said not up here I won't!"

Jesse's vehement outburst reclaimed Edward's attention. "I beg your pardon?"

"There ain't any women up here on the mountain to court."

"None at all?" Edward raised a brow at him.

"Not a one, city boy, so if you were hoping—"

"Edward," he cut in. "You agreed to call me Edward."

They finished driving through the small village and wound their way along the narrow path to where the land flattened out somewhat. It was like a vast plateau had been welded to the east side of the mountain. From here, the land stretched a few miles before adjoining the next peak.

Directly ahead of them rose a dilapidated two-story structure. Edward recognized it from the single black-and-white photo his grandfather had included in his last will and testament. They had arrived to Christmas Mountain Inn, one hundred acres of winter paradise according to the description in the will.

Or what was left of it.

The paint was peeling, and the front door was swinging open, no longer attached to its bottom hinge. Most of the shutters had fallen from the windows. One was lying on the ground below, propped against the wall. Several of the glass panes were broken, and a few were missing altogether.

Alright, then. Edward's heart sank as he surveyed the carnage sprawling before them. He finished driving his wagon to the front entrance of the inn and halted his horses. For a structure that had only lain vacant a year, it was in remarkably poor repair. It looked more like a war zone than a place intended to offer hospitality.

All that remained of the white picket fence surrounding the front yard were a few jagged stakes. Most of the slats were shattered on the ground, as if they'd been trampled by a herd of buffalo. Or a herd of elk?

Edward's gaze locked on the lone elk grazing against the west wall of the inn. He'd crossed the broken picket fence to reach whatever succulent bit of vegetation he was presently munching. The enormous creature raised his head, still chewing, and silently observed the newcomers. Edward was amazed at his complacent attitude. Most wild animals would have turned tail and run.

"That's ol' Brutus," Jessie noted in a hushed voice. "He's, more or less, a permanent guest at the inn."

From the looks of the two white horses tethered to the front porch railing, it was beginning to sound like there were plenty of uninvited guests to go around. Edward could only assume the two mounts belonged to Jesse's brothers.

As he crouched to spring to the ground, a volley of gunfire sounded. The elk bolted for the nearest copse of trees, the horses whinnied in alarm, and the snowy white horses tethered to the porch stamped their feet and reared back, tugging at their cords. The porch railing gave a disturbing creak, as if the whole thing was about to come apart.

"Whoa, there, King and Lady! Who-o-o-a-a!" Edward tightened his hands on the reins and leaned forward to pat the trembling flanks of his newly purchased team of horses. King, who had reared up to cycle his hooves in the air, careened back down on all fours. However, he continued to paw the ground as if bracing for flight.

Jesse leaped from the wagon seat and ran around the side of the porch. "Cease fire! Cease fire! You're upsetting the horses, you scallawags!"

While working valiantly to calm the horses, Edward dimly noted that Jesse had not drawn his weapon. He hoped it meant that the man wasn't in any danger from the shooters. If that was the case, though, why had they chosen to start firing the exact moment he'd arrived?

Unfortunately, he wasn't in the position to calm both his own team and the two horses still struggling to break free of the porch.

"Easy, there!" Edward called, in the hopes his voice might return some modicum of sanity in the midst of their terror.

However, another volley of shots sounded only seconds after the first ones. The white horses lunged backward in unison, whether by design or by accident, finally tearing loose from the inn. The porch railing tumbled to the ground, and the horses went haywire. They engaged in a violent, pounding dance as they tried to rid themselves of the cumbersome burden they were still tethered to. In the end, all they succeeded in doing was backing away from the inn, dragging the wooden beam with them.

The porch column it had been attached to gave an alarming groan at the missing support. Then it slowly listed outward, tearing a section of the porch roof away in the process.

Edward swiftly drove his panicked team to the far edge of the yard and leaped down to finish quieting them. His hands worked like lightning to unhitch them from the wagon. The last thing he needed was a runway pair of horses, dragging all of his newly acquired supplies pell-mell down the mountain.

"Here he is!" Jesse sang out, rounding the corner once more. He headed in Edward's direction with two burly mountain men at his side. One wore a Stetson slouched around his ears like his youngest brother. The other man had a cap of raccoon fur mashed atop his head with the tail dangling over one ear. All three men were in matching fringed suede coats.

The one in the raccoon cap had two pistols at the ready. "So you're the city slicker who thinks he's come to kick us off our land," he snarled.

Read the whole story now!
Bride for the Innkeeper
Available in eBook and paperback on Amazon + FREE on Kindle Unlimited!

Read the whole trilogy!
Bride for the Innkeeper
Bride for the Deputy
Bride for the Tribal Chief

Much love,
Jovie

Sneak Preview: Hot-Tempered Hannah

U nlike his name suggested, there was nothing angelic about Gabriel Donovan. Quite the contrary. While most men were settled down with a wife and family by his ripe old age of twenty-six, he preferred the life of a bounty hunter, tracking and rounding up men who carried a price on their heads. He extracted money and information and taught an occasional lesson to particularly deserving scoundrels when circumstances warranted it.

Most people kept their distance from him, and he was okay with that. More than okay. Making friends wasn't part of the job, and he sincerely hoped he didn't run into anyone he knew at the Pink Swan tonight. Unlike the other patrons, he wasn't looking for entertainment to brighten the endless drag of mining activities in windy Headstone, Arizona. If any of the show girls from the makeshift stage at the front of the room bothered to approach him, they'd be wasting their time. He'd purposefully chosen the dim corner table for its solitude. All he wanted was a hot meal and his own thoughts for company.

"Why, if it isn't Gunslinger Gabe," a female voice

cooed, sweet as honey and smoother than a calf's hide. She plopped a mug of watered down ale on the table, scrapping the metal cup in his direction. "I's beginning to worry you wasn't gonna show up for your Friday night supper."

"Evening, Layla." He hated her use of his nickname. Hated how the printed gazettes popping up across the West ensured he would never outride the cheeky title. It followed him from town to town like an infection. He hated it for one reason: None of his eight notorious years of quick draws and crack shots had been enough to save his partner during that fated summer night's raid.

It was a regret that weighed down his chest every second of every day like a ton of coal. It was a regret he would carry to his grave.

He nodded at the waitress who leaned one hand on the small round table with chipped black paint.

"Well, what's it going to be this time, cowboy?" Her dark eyes snapped with a mixture of interest and impatience. "Bean stew? Mutton pie? As purty as your eyes are, I got other tables to wait on, you know."

The compliment never failed to disgust him. Along with his angelic name, he'd been told more times than he cared to count that he'd been gifted with innocent features. If he heard another word about his clear, lake-blue eyes that inspired trust, he would surely vomit.

"Surprise me." He hoped to change the subject. Both entrees sounded equally good to him. He was hungry enough to eat the pewter serving ware, if she didn't hurry up with his order.

Layla's movements were slow as sap rolling down the bark of a maple tree. "If it's a surprise you're looking for…." She swayed a step closer.

"Bring me both," he said quickly. "The stew and the pie. I haven't eaten since this morning."

"Fine." The single word was infused with a world of derisive disappointment. A few steps into her stormy retreat, she spun around. Anger rippled in waves across her heart-shaped face. "I know what you really want."

"You do?" The question grated out past his lips before he could recall the words. Sarcastic and challenging. It had been a rough day. The last thing he needed was a saloon wench to whip out her crystal ball and presume to know anything about his life. Or his longings. No one this side of the grave could fill the void in his heart.

"I sure do, cowboy." She was back in front of him before he could blink, her scarlet dress shimmering with her movements. "An' I can show you a real special time. Something you ain't never gonna find on no supper menu."

He didn't figure any good would come of trying to explain that his heart belonged to a ghost. Wracking his brain for a sensible way to end their conversation without offending her further, he stared drearily at his mug. There was no quickening of his breathing around any women these days. No increased thump of his heartbeat. Not like there had been with Hannah. His dead partner. Or Hot-Tempered Hannah, as she'd been known throughout the West.

Then again, maybe he wasn't completely dead yet on the inside. He felt a stirring in the sooty, blackened, charred recesses of his brain as his memories of her sprang back to life. Memories that refused to die.

His mind swiftly conjured up all five feet three inches of her boyishly slender frame stuffed in men's breeches along with the tumultuous swing of red hair she'd refused to pin up like a proper lady. Nor could he forget the taunting tilt of her head and the voice that turned from sweet to sassy in a heartbeat, a voice that had been silenced forever due to his failure to reach their rendezvous in time.

Lord help him, but he was finally feeling something alright — a sharp gushing hole of pain straight through the chest. He mechanically reached for his glass and downed the rest of his ale in one harsh gulp.

"Well, I'll be!" The waitress peered closer at him, at first with amazement then with growing irritation. "I've been around long enough to know when a body's pining for someone else."

What? Am I that transparent? His brows shot up and he stared back, thoroughly annoyed at her intrusive badgering.

Layla was the first to lower her eyes. "Guess I'll get back to work, since you're of no mind to chat." Her frustration raised her voice to a higher pitch. "I was jes' trying to be friendly, you unsociable cad. I'll try not to burn your pie or spill your soup, since that's all you be wanting." Her voice scorched his ears as she pivoted in a full circle and stormed in the direction of the kitchen.

He stared after her, wishing he could call her back but knowing his apology wouldn't make her feel any better. A woman scorned was a deadly thing indeed. He could only hope she didn't poison his supper.

He hunched his shoulders over his corner table and went back to reminiscing about his dead partner. Known as Hot-Tempered Hannah throughout Arizona, she'd stolen his heart with a single kiss then threatened to shoot him if he ever tried to steal another.

He had yet to get over her. Hadn't looked at another woman since. She was three months in the grave, and he was nowhere near moving on with his life.

Layla stomped back in his direction twice. Once to refill his mug and several minutes later to dump his tray on the table with such a clatter that a few droplets of stew spilled over the edge of the bowl.

"A man at one of the faro tables paid me to deliver you a message," she snapped. "He wants you to stick around 'til he's finished dealing. Says he needs to speak with you 'bout somethin' important."

The drowsy contentedness settling in Gabe's bones from the hot meal sharpened back to full awareness. He paused in the act of lifting a spoonful of stew to his mouth. "Which man?"

She pointed to the nearest gaming table. "Over there. The one dealing."

Technically, the man was shuffling, but he pushed back his Stetson an inch and deliberately nodded a greeting in response to their curious stares. Gabe didn't recognize him. They were dressed much the same, albeit Gabe hadn't bothered to remove his trench coat like the other man had.

His keen bounty hunter eyes zeroed in on the ridge of concealed weapons beneath the man's vest. Most people wouldn't have noticed, but Gabe wasn't most people. He was well paid to notice everything around him. The things people wanted him to notice and the things they preferred he didn't.

Those same sensory nodes told him Layla was still present, though she was standing behind him not making a peep. His gaze remained fixed on his summoner. "Does this faro dealer have a name?"

She sniffed. "He didn't say, and I ain't takin' extra to find out. He's working a little too hard for my tastes to fit in, if you know what I mean."

Gabe knew exactly what she meant and was surprised enough at her perception to spare her a glance. He reached in his pocket, and she tensed. He slid an extra bill in her direction across the scratched up tabletop. Something told him she could use the money. "Thanks for passing on the gentleman's message."

The frown on her lacquered lips eased. "Maybe some time you and I can visit a little longer, gunslinger?" She batted her lashes at him.

He highly doubted it — ever. "Dinner tastes wonderful. I thank you for that as well." He returned his hand to his soup spoon and his attention to the faro dealer. Something told him he was about to receive a new bounty assignment.

Layla lingered a few moments longer but finally left him on a drawn-out sigh of resignation.

He ate quickly while observing the card game. In seconds, he determined the game was rigged. Unlike most tables where the odds generally leaned in the banker's favor, this table broke even every few rounds. The intervals were entirely too regular to be coincidental. If Gabe's suspicions were correct, the faro dealer wasn't making a penny. *Very odd.* He chewed his mutton pie more slowly, watching the man.

When the man looked up between rounds, he allowed their gazes to clash once more. A nod from him had a new faro dealer rushing forward to claim the oval table with its green baize covering. The man closed down his rigged game, tucked his crooked gaming box beneath his arm, and sauntered in Gabe's direction amidst the cries for higher stakes from the newest dealer on the floor.

Gabe took in the man's tousled brown hair, even stride, and confident air. His senses told him the man was on a mission but not out for blood. Nevertheless, he kept a hand on his holster as the man stopped beside his table.

"May I join you?" The thick northeastern accent tickled his curiosity further.

A Bostonian, if Gabe was a betting man. Which he

wasn't where money was concerned. He dipped his head in agreement without breaking eye contact.

The man took a seat, cradling the card box between his hands on the table in front of him. He was far more at ease than most men tended to be in the presence of Gunslinger Gabe. His long fingers were scarred on one hand, puckered and mottled a permanent shade of salmon as if he'd held his hand in a fire a few moments too long.

"I need your help." His words were simple and quietly spoken, not the usual hard-nosed beginning to a proper bounty negotiation. His tone was missing the sharp bite of revenge or the frantic pace of a man in a hurry.

Gabe leaned forward. "Most reputable men introduce themselves."

A half-grin softened the man's features another degree as he signaled Layla. "Most reputable men are fools. I'd much rather start a conversation by wetting my whistle."

Gabe's hand tightened on his holster. "And I'd rather start with a name."

The man shrugged. "Have it your way, gunslinger, but I'll have more to say if I wet my tongue first."

"I prefer to know who I'm drinking with."

"Fair enough." The man's grin widened as if he was pleased with what he was hearing. "I run my faro table under the name of Sharp Masterson."

"And your real name is?"

"Must you ask so many questions, gunslinger?"

"Most men prefer to keep me talking."

The man laughed aloud this time and reached for the drink Layla offered. Taking a sip, he eyed Gabe over the rim. "Colt Branson, since you insist on knowing."

Gabe shook his head. "Not ringing a bell. Don't suppose you go by any other handles?"

"Nope. I keep a low profile, but the second name I gave you is real enough."

The man's direct manner impressed Gabe as honest. It wasn't accompanied by the usual twitching and glancing away of a person with something to hide.

"I'm listening." Anxious to finish filling the clawing hole in his belly, he resumed eating his mutton pie with gusto. The sooner he finished eating, the sooner he could get moving again. He'd made many enemies in his line of business. As a rule, he never stayed too long in any one town.

Colt held his gaze with unwavering intensity. "As I said before, I need your help. More precisely, The Boomtown Mail Order Brides Company needs your help."

Boomtown what? Gabe waited a few heartbeats before attempting to swallow the bite of pie in his mouth. As it was, he had to choke it down and cough to clear his throat. If he had any laughter left in his soul, he would have laughed. "Clearly you're confused about what line of business I'm in, Mr. Branson."

The man waved his hand carelessly. "You can drop the mister. Just call me Colt. And you're exactly the kind of man I need for this job."

Gabe was only half listening as he finished up his last bite of pie and nursed the remaining swig or two of his ale. He swirled it around the bottom of his glass before taking a sip.

"We've lost contact with one of our brides-to-be."

Your problem. Not mine. Gabe raised his brows, incredulous that Colt had singled him out to share his sorry tale. Rescuing damsels in distress was a skill he simply didn't possess. Hot-Tempered Hannah was proof enough of that. A fresh splinter of pain ricocheted through his chest. He emptied his mug, hardly realizing he'd pressed a palm to his heart where his ache was the worse.

Colt's gaze followed his hand. "You and I both know the West isn't a safe place for young, marriageable women. Why so many of them flock to fill the ever-growing pile of mail order bride applications is thoroughly beyond me. Even the toughest among them don't always survive. Better to stay in more civilized cities back East."

Gabe wished the man would hurry up and get to his point. *Even the toughest...don't always survive.* The conversation was treading dangerously close to Hannah's tragic demise, making his trigger finger itch something powerful.

Colt abruptly shoved aside his dealer box to lean closer. He lowered his voice, but it accentuated rather than lessened the fierceness of his words. "My own sister, may she rest in peace, was one of those eager mail order brides. I'll never know why she decided to become one. Probably speculate myself into an early grave. Maybe it was because she wasn't much use with a needle and thread. Or maybe it was because anytime I caught her in the kitchen, I tended to skip dinner that night. But she could ride a horse like a demon, and she could hold her own with a gun." He shook his head admiringly, then sobered. "In the end, gunslinger, neither of those things could save MaryAnne from the cruelty of the man she married."

"What happened?" Gabe both wanted to know and didn't want to know.

"Her late husband claimed it was a stagecoach robbery that went south." He balled his hands into fists on the tabletop. "Said they were in the wrong place at the wrong time, but that doesn't explain the fire or the—" He fiercely bit off whatever else he was about to say and took a deep breath. "The stage company was kind enough to send her remains home, so we could lay her to rest."

It was a tragic tale, yet Gabe found himself envying the man his closure. As for himself, he'd never received a body to bury, only the news that Hot-Tempered Hannah was dead. He bit down on the inside of his cheek. Hard. Enough to draw the coppery tang of blood across his tongue. "I'm sorry for your loss but with all due respect, I don't see how any of this applies to me." Harsh but true.

Colt's upper lip curled. "I don't believe that for a second. Don't tell me you've never asked your Maker for a do-over."

"A do-over?"

"A second chance."

Leave it alone, mister. Gabe's hand literally tingled with the itch to draw and fire. Colt Branson clearly had no idea what dangerous ground he was treading. "I have no idea what you're talking about."

"Of course, you do, and that's why you're going to help me find Heloise."

"Who?" Gabe choked back a snarl. Maybe the man was a bit touched in the head. It was the only explanation for his foolish persistence in toying with a gunslinger.

"She's one of our mail order brides. We should have received her letter by now, notifying us of her safe arrival to Headstone; but there've been no letters. No mention of her among the other brides we placed in neighboring towns. Nothing. She just—" He snapped his fingers. "Up and vanished!" His skin beneath his tan had paled, and he sounded truly distraught.

Gabe scrubbed a hand down his jaw, wishing he could offer a ray of comfort to the troubled faro dealer, touched in the noggin' or not. "Mail runs slow in some parts of the country. Maybe you should give it more time."

"We require our brides to write their letters before they

leave Boston. All each of them has to do when she reaches her destination is date it and mail it."

"So have a chat with the post master."

For the first time in their short conversation, Colt's mouth gave an ugly downward twist of irritation. "Come on, gunslinger. I arrived here a week ago. Tracking down that fellow was the first thing on my list, and I was prepared to rip out his toenails one by one if need be to jog his memory of her. Except the poor chap seems to have vanished as well. I asked around town about him, but they said he was involved in some sort of stage coach accident. They found remnants of the carriage and wheels strewn down the side of a cliff but no bodies."

So the hopeful bride was missing. Tough times. She could be anywhere. Holed up in the mountains or chained inside a brothel, her virtue a distant memory. Anger churned in Gabe's gut. Unfortunately, things like that happened on occasion in the wild West. Some women just weren't meant to travel to these dusty towns of lonely, lust-crazed, and sometimes desperate men. Not everyone could hold their own or go out guns a-blazing like Hot-Tempered Hannah had.

Colt's missing Heloise was dead or as good as dead. Gabe wasn't a doomsday kind of guy; he was just facing the facts. Why then did questions start to bubble up his throat about the unfortunate woman?

"How long has she been missing, and what did she look like?" he blurted. Was she pretty enough to attract the attention of a madame? Had Colt bothered to scope out the brothels in the nearest towns?

He didn't know why he was asking. He certainly had no intention of helping Colt and his mail order bride company. Not for any price. He was too afraid of what he might find on the other end. The carnage. And death.

Too afraid of failing to save another woman.

Colt's shoulders relaxed a fraction at the barrage of questions, though his forearms remained resting on the edge of the table. The music in the background transitioned from a swinging ballad to something rowdier. The room grew louder. And hotter. And more suffocating.

Gabe could only pray he and Colt were about finished with their miserable discussion. Lord help him, he needed some fresh air.

"The last time any of us saw Heloise was two months ago when she boarded her train. She was wearing a simple brown taffeta gown." Colt's face settled into another half-grin. "When she first came to us, she had the kind of red hair no comb can tame, though the Boomtown matrons on our staff tried their best. They couldn't tame her mouth either. Or erase the bruises way down deep in her eyes. Impressed me as one of those wild little fillies who's seen things she didn't care to talk about. Our other brides-to-be tried to befriend her, but she mostly kept to herself. Kind of haunted like. Not that she would have fit in with them anyway." He gave a long, drown-out sigh of regret. "Reminded me of my sister, MaryAnne. She wasn't soft or gently spoken. Not skilled in any womanly arts that I could tell. She didn't look all that comfortable in a dress either, come to think of it. But she was full of fire no scoundrel has the right to put out before her time."

Colt's description of the young woman made Gabe swallow hard. Heloise sounded like Hot-Tempered Hannah all over again. A free spirit. An untamed heart with a thirst for adventure. And deader than dead if she'd already been missing for two full months.

There was no way Colt Branson could possibly know every one of his words sank into his listener like a gunshot. By the time the faro dealer was through describing his missing bride-to-be, it was all Gabe could do to remain sitting upright in his chair. His chest and torso were so riddled with emotional holes, he wouldn't have been the least shocked to feel the drip of blood on the hands he had fisted on his thighs.

Another woman was dead. It was an old, tired tale. Hell simply wasn't big enough for all the scum-eating renegades crawling the landscape these days. The gold-hungry, devil-may-care, barely human creatures who lived for little more than the next thrill. They were affection-starved and utterly depraved. Men who couldn't remember what it was like to be in the presence of a real lady. Men who wouldn't hesitate to take advantage of one, given half a chance.

"I'm sorry. I can't help you." Colt could shower his ears with all the piteous pleas in the world, but it wouldn't bring the missing bride one step closer to being found. It would be easier to locate a five-leaf clover in a field of December snow. Heloise was gone. The sooner Colt accepted the fact, the better.

"Can't or won't?" Colt snarled, gripping the edges of the table with both hands.

"Can't. Won't. Does it matter? She's gone." Gabe pushed away from the table and stood, desperate for a mouthful of fresh air before his lungs exploded.

"Is that what you want to believe?" Colt stood as well. "Because you buried your partner's body like I buried my sister's?"

How in tarnation did Colt know so much about his past when they'd never met before tonight? "Watch yourself, Sharp." Gabe's hand slid to his gun holster again. Hannah had been burnt alive; there had been nothing left to bury. Something told him Colt knew this, too.

"Did you?" Colt pressed. "Because if you did, then I'm wasting my breath by telling you the Boomtown Mail

Order Brides Company received a ransom note for Heloise."

Meaning the poor woman might still be alive after all. And probably wishing she was dead…

"How much?" Gabe gritted through his teeth, making an inhuman effort to keep his voice down.

"Two grand."

It was a fortune. More than most lawmen made in a year and bigger than any other single bounty Gabe had earned. "Why so much?"

"Her abductor didn't say, but he seemed awfully concerned about listing every known name in the ransom note that Heloise might have ever used. Hester. Holly." He paused, dipping his head to peer beneath Gabe's Stetson. "Hannah."

For a moment, Gabe couldn't hear past the buzzing in his head. Hester and Holly were among the many aliases Hot-Tempered Hannah had used on their string of joint assignments as bounty hunters.

"Oh, and here's the sketch another one of our mail order brides made of Heloise the night before she traveled West to meet her intended groom." Colt reached inside his vest and withdrew a charcoal portrait. He held it out.

Gabe reached for the small square of canvas and his insides went numb. He took a stumbling step towards the table and sank back into his seat. A coldness like he'd never known before spread through his chest. The sketch wasn't a perfect likeness, but it was close enough. There was no mistaking the challenging tilt of the woman's face or the determined set to her chin.

It was Hannah or someone who resembled her enough to pass as her twin, which made no sense. Hannah had never mentioned a sister. She'd never mentioned having family at all, for that matter.

The sketch slid from his nerveless fingers to the table. He slowly leaned forward on his elbows to grip his head in both hands. He closed his eyes, uncaring that his movements sent his Stetson tumbling to the floor. He fisted his hair roots until the tearing pressure on his skull rivaled the screaming questions in his brain.

There was another possibility — one that filled him with frantic joy and raging agony — that, by some miracle, Hannah was alive.

If it were true, it could only mean one thing. She'd faked her death. But why? Had she done it to double-cross him and take their final bounty purse for herself? Was it possible the woman he'd loved with every ounce of his life had secretly despised him in return? So much so that she'd been that desperate to get rid of him?

Gabe's heart felt like it was festering with a thousand blisters. The worst part about the possibility that Hannah was still alive was the fact she was trying to marry another man.

He didn't know how long he sat there. It could have been minutes or hours before the red-hot lava of anger finally burst through his numbness. Heat shot through his bloodstream and gave him the strength to lower his hands and meet Colt's concerned gaze. He needed answers. No, he desperately craved them, and there was only one way to get them. "I'm going to find her."

He would track her down, haul her double-crossing hide back to Headstone, and demand answers to every question scorching the walls of his soul. She owed him that at least.

"I know you will." Colt produced a folded parchment and slid it across the table in his direction. "Here's our contract. We'll cover your travel expenses, and there will be a sizable reward when you return her to us. Not anywhere near as big as the ransom note but enough to make it worth your while."

Gabe wasn't taking anyone's money. Not for this job. Finding Hannah was strictly personal. He started to crumple the contract, but Colt's eyelids narrowed to warning slits.

"You'll not lay eyes on the ransom note until you sign my contract."

The maniacal thought ran through Gabe's head that he could shoot Colt's knees out from under him and torture him into giving him what he wanted, but Colt didn't exactly impress him as a man who would buckle quickly or easily under pressure. And Gabe didn't have time to quibble. Heloise had already been missing two months. The clock was ticking.

When Colt handed him a pen, he scrawled a hasty signature. "Tell me everything you know."

"I will as soon as you raise your right hand and repeat your oath of allegiance to the Gallant Rescue Society."

Gallant who? Never mind. It didn't matter. Gabe's insides churned with determination as he recited the oath, hardly registering the words coming from his mouth. "I hereby solemnly pledge my gun and my honor to the Gallant Rescue Society…so help me God."

Like a stallion pawing at the ground, he was frothing at the mouth to break into a gallop on his mission. The only thing in the world that mattered anymore was finding Hannah. He'd start his search in the Yellow Diamond Mine on the outskirts of Headstone. It was where she'd supposedly burnt to death during a premature dynamite explosion in an underground tunnel. A place of business he swore he'd never return to. The home of a gang of squatters who wanted him dead.

Hope you enjoyed the excerpt from
Mail Order Brides Rescue Series 1:
Hot-Tempered Hannah
Available now in eBook, paperback, and Kindle Unlimited on
Amazon.

This is a complete 12-book series.
Read them all!
Hot-Tempered Hannah
Book 2: Cold-Feet Callie
Book 3: Fiery Felicity
Book 4: Misunderstood Meg
Book 5: Dare-Devil Daisy
Book 6: Outrageous Olivia
Book 7: Jinglebell Jane
Book 8: Absentminded Amelia
Book 9: Bookish Belinda
Book 10: Tenacious Trudy
Book 11: Meddlesome Madge
Book 12: Mismatched MaryAnne
Box Set #1: Books 1-4
Box Set #2: Books 5-8
Box Set #3: Books 9-12

Much love,
Jovie

Also by Jovie

For the most up-to-date printable list of my sweet historical books:

Click here

or go to:

https://www.jografford.com/joviegracebooks

For the most up-to-date printable list of my sweet contemporary books:

Click here

or go to:

https://www.JoGrafford.com/books

About Jovie

Jovie Grace is an Amazon bestselling author of sweet and inspirational historical romance books full of faith, family, and second chances. She also writes sweet contemporary romance as Jo Grafford.

Free Book!

Visit www.JoGrafford.com to sign up for my New Release Newsletter and receive a FREE copy of one of my sweet romance stories!

1.) Follow on Amazon!

https://www.amazon.com/author/joviegrace

2.) Join Cuppa Jo Readers!

https://www.facebook.com/groups/CuppaJoReaders

3.) Follow on Bookbub!

https://www.bookbub.com/authors/jovie-grace

4.) Follow on Facebook!

https://www.facebook.com/JovieGraceBooks

Made in the USA
Columbia, SC
21 June 2022

62036775R00102